DING DONG BELL
DEATH IN A STAIRWELL

FRAN HAGAMAN

Requests for such permission should be addressed to:
Loch Wohl Press,
78 Erie Stree.
Shreveport, LA 71106

Hagaman, Frances E.
        Ding Dong Bell, Death in a Stairwell

Cover Design: M. G. Saloff
Layout: J. L. Saloff

Print book ISBN: 978-0-9749649-2-8
Ebook ISBN: 978-0-9749649-3-5

First edition

In loving memory and friendship to:
Joseph E. Manno, Ph. D.
Professor and Chief of Clinical Toxicology
Department of Emergency Medicine
Louisiana State University School of Medicine
in Shreveport

Thanks, Joe, for suggesting tetrodotoxin.

ACKNOWLEDGMENTS

The author gratefully acknowledges the kind assistance she has received from the following:

Joe and Barbara Manno – forensic toxicologists

Pat Matson – editing assistance

Dr. Lee Morgan

Mark Saloff – cover design

Jamie Saloff – book layout and design

DING DONG BELL
DEATH IN A STAIRWELL

FRAN HAGAMAN

LOCH WOHL PRESS

ONE

"Whew! Men!" said Clare.

"What's up?" said Trish, a slim brunette, turning from her computer screen.

It was early afternoon at the Gulf Coast Medical Center where both women were professors of Psychiatry.

"Nothing I hope, and I pity the woman who's around when it is. That guy was about to get a hard-on during the physical exam."

"What are you talking about, Clare?"

"That kid; actually he's in his thirties. A few minutes ago, I entered him in the anxiety study. He's hung like a horse."

"Maybe his women like him that way." Trish smiled, her blue gray eyes twinkling in amusement.

"I find that hard to believe. Talk about anxious. He was trembling like a leaf."

"Enough of this discussion. What else is going on?"

"Us being in a male-dominated department, you're about the only person I can even mention such things as this to."

"Clare, maybe your blonde hair and perfume — I notice you have on Dolce & Gabanna today — made him anxious."

"Oh, Trish, I doubt that."

"You never know what rings someone's bell."

Trish swiveled her chair to one side and arose in a quick graceful movement. "I need to check in with Sheila, so toddle on to your consultation rounds."

Sheila, Trish's red-haired stressed-out secretary, occupied

the main department office around the corner a scant five yards away.

Trish headed for her overflowing mailbox.

"Hi, Sheila. What's the word?"

"Cooking with Crisco, Dr. Trish. Have a good morning at Mental Health?"

"Yes, indeed; no patients on my book showed up, so I checked email, a couple of blogs, Googled a bit, and read an on-line case conference. On the way back to the Medical Center, I noticed something building up weather wise to the southwest toward the Gulf. We may have a thundershower in a bit."

"Hope it doesn't happen before I leave. I left my windows down."

Trish removed the stack of assorted mail from her box and sorted through it, giving only a cursory glance before tossing most in the trash can at her feet. A few first class letters and messages in her hand, Trish continued, "Think I'll walk around to the Chairman's office for a little chat with Martha."

"Be kind. She's stressed out today."

"What about?"

Sheila rolled her chair across the office to retrieve an incoming FAX.

"Oh, something about the Dean calling for Dr. Parker, and Parker told her to say he wasn't in and the Dean knew that he was. So she was caught in the middle, fibbing for her boss, but in big trouble with the big boss." Sheila rolled her chair back and tilted it.

"That could have been handled better," said Trish frowning.

Sheila arose placing her hands akimbo on her hips and continued.

"Dr. Trish, does he really need to do all that traveling? He's gone more than he is here."

"I can't say for sure, Sheila. He does speak at lots of meetings, but I think he simply likes to travel and looks for opportunity as his predecessors did. Maybe he has a mistress or two in some of those cities."

Grinning, Sheila quipped, "Dr. Trish! Shame on you!"

"I didn't mean to say that. A mere Freudian slip. He probably has problems getting it up. I bet he never passes up Viagra samples. Let me go cheer Martha up."

"Dr. Trish, you are so bad. I hope no one else hears you talking that way."

"They won't unless you rat, Sheila."

With a grin and a slight swagger, Trish exited the office and strode down the hall, her shoes squeaking and clicking on the terrazzo floor.

A few minutes later as Martha and Trish had their heads together, discussing strategy for handling Martha's dilemma, when a loud boom of thunder penetrated the windowless office. Both women jumped and Martha said, "Check on that, will you, Dr. Trish? The window in the stairwell at the end of the hall looks out the other way from those in the seminar room. Maybe you can see something from there."

The fire exit stairwell located in a rear corner of the building was seldom entered, because it wasn't suitable for shortcuts. Below the psychiatry floor, there were only entries from the rear library stacks. The doors locked upon entering the stairwell; and unless someone came to the rescue, the only way to the outside was at the very bottom of the stairs. When opened, the emergency door there set off an alarm equal in intensity to cats mating. That stairwell was a dead area of the building. It served as an infirmary for the office staff's potted plants set out on a windowsill for an occasional dose of light. However, its most frequent use was to check on weather conditions.

The heavy door, with its small eye-level reinforced glass window, resisted as Trish pushed to open it.

"God, is this thing stuck? Great, for a fire exit; can't get the frigging door open," she muttered as she put her shoulder to it while turning the handle.

The door gave way and she stepped around it into the stairwell.

"Holy shit! It's a damn body," exclaimed Trish.

The young Asian woman, a crumpled heap on the floor in a white lab coat with a Biochemistry label on the breast pocket, had prevented the easy opening of the door. Trish knelt and lifted one eyelid a bit.

"Pupil fixed and dilated," whispered Trish.

As she checked for a carotid pulse, she continued under her breath, "She's dead; stone cold dead. Hell, what's this?"

The young woman's silky black hair fell back from her neck revealing a small blue heart-shaped tattoo on her neck behind her left ear. On the floor beside the body lay a slip of paper with a phone number she recognized as Clare's personal office number.

Trish bolted from the stairwell into the nearest office.

"Call Security! There's a corpse in the stairwell! No need for a crash cart. She's dead for certain."

❁

TWO

The news of the discovery spread at warp speed through-out the Medical Center. This was the first incident of this magnitude since a female graduate student was raped and thrown off the top floor of the Research Building while it was under construction several years earlier. That killer was now serving a life sentence up state at Parchman Prison.

Trish walked down the hall to her office and sat stunned at her desk. She realized she had picked up the slip of paper with her dear friend Clare's number on it.

Moments later Sheila entered the office with a look of concern.

"You okay, Dr. Trish?"

"I think so, Sheila. You heard?"

"Yeah, saw the police walk by my office. You found the body?"

"Damnation, yes. I was going to look out the window to check on the thunder Martha and I heard." Body rigid, she rotated her chair in a complete circle.

"How long had she been there?"

"Hard to say, but there was no doubt she was dead. No pulse, and cool to touch."

"You touched her?" Sheila put her hand to her open mouth in horror.

"Sheila, I had to check for a pulse and you can't do that by looking, and the funniest, not funny, but most interesting thing is she had a little blue heart tattoo on her neck behind her left ear, same shape and color as one a research volunteer who was rejected for the anxiety study had a couple of weeks ago." Trish pulled her fingers through her dark hair and rubbed the back of her neck.

"Maybe that's the latest thing? A fad, like a certain kind of shoes or piece of jewelry, Dr. Trish?"

Sheila sat on top of a pile of papers stacked on a chair in Trish's overstuffed office.

"Could be. Somehow I don't get that impression. I'm going to wait here for the police to come. Send them around if they show up in your office. Without a doubt, everyone in this part of the building will be questioned."

Sheila arose to leave. "No problem, Dr. Trish."

"One more thing, Sheila, do you remember seeing any Asian staff or students walking by your office? The glass wall in your office and your door open give you a good view of traffic."

"No, none caught my attention. So many walk by doing their walkabout exercise, I pay no mind unless they stick their head in my door and speak."

"She was such a little thing, Sheila."

Trish's throat and chest tightened and her breathing became shallow. "Like a little white bird in that lab coat, with coal black hair in a page-boy bob, shiny as a crow. There was an ID badge and access card on a strap around her neck."

"Her coat label said Biochemistry?" asked Sheila as she turned to leave.

Trish nodded and bit her lower lip. "Yes, and we're a long way from that department. I seldom see any of those graduate students past the main bank of elevators. Say, Sheila, ask around what's the latest in tattoos, will you?"

Sheila rolled her eyes.

"Sure thing, Dr. Trish. I better get back to my office and the phones. Bev, our current student clerk, will be having a fit answering them since she doesn't think it is her job."

"Close the door, will you? And turn off the overhead light. This banker's lamp on my desk is sufficient for now."

Trish swiveled the desk chair to reach the radio/cd player on the credenza behind the desk. The soothing sound of a Chopin nocturne wafted over her as she leaned back, closing her eyes, and gently rocked.

Trish knew a dialog was beginning between the critical and fun-loving parts of her psyche.

Now you've done it again.

What?

Stumbled on another corpse. Now, why has this happened once more?

Just bad luck, I guess.

Oh, no! You can't get away with that. Remember when you discovered Hilda Rasberry's body. What was the reason?

Oh, you mean doing something someone asks me to check on?

Yep! Was it your idea to check on the weather?

No, it was Martha's, and boy, did she jump when we heard the thunder.

Some people might check, see a body, realize the person was dead, and let someone else report it. Ever think of that?

No, but it is possible that my fingerprints are on the door-knob anyway. I was struggling so to open the damn door.

Did you see a weapon?

No, I didn't look that close. What makes you ask that? Maybe she was caught by the door and died of some attack like a cardiac arrest because no one heard her knocking. Or maybe she went into the stairwell from the library stacks for a snort of something like coke and it was extra strong and she arrested. We've seen that in the ER more than once in a young person.

Oh shut up! Sometimes I get so fed up with you and your ideas.

As Trish concluded her internal dialog there was a knock at the door.

"Come on in. It's open."

Trish turned her chair and arose as a clean-cut man with gray eyes opened the door and hesitated.

"Dr. McLeod?"

"Officers, come in and have a seat. Put those papers on the floor and please, call me Dr. Trish."

"My pleasure. My name is Bill Swanson and this is Detective Dick Benson."

As he sat, the detective said, "I believe we had some contact a year or two back on another case, didn't we?"

"Yes, it was Hilda Rasberry. I found her body in the bathtub at the Mental Health Clinic."

"That case was solved, as I remember with your input. How did you happen to discover this young woman's body?"

Swanson surveyed the office before making eye contact again.

Trish related what happened and how she was checking on the weather.

"By the way, was it raining when you came inside?" she asked.

"Only a sprinkle," replied Swanson. "Now, did you know this young woman?"

Not one for social graces is he?

"No, sir. I don't remember seeing her around the school — say in the Deli or on the elevators. But that doesn't mean much. We have hundreds of students if you include all types. Many are primarily in the hospital and don't venture into this part of the Medical Center."

"Ever?"

"I couldn't say for certain. The library is nearby. If there was a crunch for space, possibly one of our seminar rooms or a classroom might be used. Many office staff pass down this hall on their walkabouts because it is on the route to the Medical School, where one can walk the farthest without opening doors. Mostly though, we use the space ourselves. Did she die right there, Detective?"

"I'm not at liberty to share my view at this time. If she did, we'll know after the post."

"My God!" Trish drew in a sharp breath. "I walked past there several times yesterday. I didn't notice anything."

"The entrance to that stairwell is set back in an alcove," said Detective Swanson. "There was no reason for you to check unless there was someone knocking to get out, or you were checking on the weather as you did today."

"You are right, but the thought still gives me the creeps. Will you want my fingerprints again?" asked Trish.

"Not necessary; you're on file. Thank you for your time today."

Swanson arose, nodded to his partner, who replaced the papers from the floor to the chair, and, making another slow survey of the room with his eyes, turned to leave.

"I hope we haven't taken too much of your time."

"No problem. You can leave the door ajar for now, Detective."

❀

THREE

Trish swiveled her chair facing away from the door, kicked off her high-heeled sandals, tilted back, and rubbed the back of her neck as yet another internal chat began.

What do we think of him now?

Same as before; there's something about that guy that rubs me the wrong way. Can't put my finger on it.

He's still a spiffy dresser; nice khakis, navy blazer, and his tie wasn't half bad.

Half bad! It was terrible. Those were little green lizards on it.

Are you sure? I didn't notice. I thought they were leaves.

They were lizards. Believe me, your better half, maybe simply your other half, your alter ego. Can we stay out of this?

You've two babies and a husband now. Don't go messing with this.

What do you mean?

Let's not get involved like the other time you found a dead body.

I'm not. But what if it is murder?

We don't know how she died, and we're not involved.

Not yet. Look though, you have to admit. It's a curiosity.

Curiosity, that was a major part of Trish's makeup — curious about the mind, curious about why people act and feel the way they do, and curious about the things they do.

Not that she wanted to sleuth crime. She was totally willing to leave that up to professionals.

Trish looked up at the ceiling tiles at a stain that resembled an obscene Rorschach and resumed her internal dialog.

Are you sure it's not more than that?

Do we — or do we not — get a rush from things like this?

A rush? Like good sex? No way. There's no comparison.

Boy, you're defensive about that. Wonder why?

Now look who's curious, Ms. Alter Ego.

We both live in this same body and mind, so to speak. Both aspects of our personality, even our logical lineal thinking part, understand that the human species is capable of almost any violent or illegal act.

It's that some of us are a little more defended against our inner base instincts.

You mean civilized?

You could call it that, but some would call it 'by the grace of God."

Can we stop this internal chit-chat?

Not yet. Think a pattern for violence starts early?

Hell, yes. Ever hear the child psychiatrist talk about how little bitty kids have to get the last word in, or how vindictive even three- or four-year-olds can be? You look at those children and some basic emotional needs haven't been met.

May be the case with a lot of them, but what about the crack babies?

Oh, that's another can of worms.

We must stop this chatter now.

Trish closed her self-talk as she sat up, slipped on her shoes, and picked up the ringing phone.

It was Steven her husband checking to see if their long-planned trip to Hong Kong was on. The dead woman was on the news, and he hoped Trish's discovery of her body would not require a cancellation of their long-anticipated trip.

❁

FOUR

"I've always wanted a cornflower blue sapphire, but I never dreamed they came in all these sizes and shapes," said Trish as she fingered the large display produced by the tiny Chinese man. He was dressed in a black suit, white shirt, red tie in a four-hand knot, and had a crisp, red, silk carnation boutonnière handsomely defined under the harsh fluorescent shop lights.

"Do you have anything better? Show us your good stuff," said Steven.

"Of course, sir," and the little man disappeared behind a beaded screen to bring forth yet another tray of sapphires larger than the previous five trays Steven had asked for. With a smooth motion, the shop owner placed it on the counter for Trish. Steven was relentless in requiring yet another tray, saying in an authoritative manner," Show us your good stuff."

Trish a little embarrassed, "Don't you think this is the good stuff?"

"Maybe not, Trish. Look at what he's been bringing out. Each tray is better than the last and the jewels keep getting larger."

"Steven, are you sure these are real? This last tray look as big as bird eggs."

"This jeweler comes recommended. The shop is supposed to be one of the best in Hong Kong. The owner is somehow related to a missionary family who came fifty years ago whose descendants stayed and went into business instead of continuing mission work."

"If finding this place is any indication of how great he is, I am not too sure. Remember we had to get someone to bring us here?" Trish continued in a whisper. "That first attempt from the business card was a total flop."

"At least we found the street off that main shopping avenue in Kowloon, and we even had the store numbers in sight — then poof! Our number wasn't there. Only a crack in the wall between two buildings. Shades of Harry Potter. How weird was that?"

"Pretty weird, Trish. Maybe we had the wrong street, or there are two streets with the same name? I would not put it past them in Hong Kong. When the man from the hotel brought us, the name on the street outside was the same as on the card.

"And how is it that this fantastic jewelry store that you heard of all the way back home in Mississippi is like some shady, hole-in-the wall outfit?"

"Maybe that is the way they do things over here. I have to admit I had a few hairs rise on the back of my neck when I heard passwords in some strange language and went through three locked doors and up those narrow, twisted stairs that squeaked. I pray there isn't a fire. At least they could have put a light in the stairwell."

"And stranger still once we've been in this inner sanctum — if you will — it seems like a normal shop, well-lighted, with other normal-appearing customers,"

At that point in their whispered conversation, Trish sighed as the clerk opened the last case to reveal a cornflower blue sapphire the size of a bird egg.

"I can't believe this. Look, Steven."

"Wow! That hums for you, and you were acting negative about my saying show us the good stuff."

"You are sooo right; it is singing to me, but it is on the large size for a ring. But I want it, I want it, I want it," Trish chanted like a kid.

"Don't let that bother you. It will make a nice paper

weight," joked Steven." I promised you something extra special."

As she picked up and rotated the jewel in her hand, a warmth and tingle moved up into her arm.

"This has a life of its own, Steven."

"Very special stone; very special history," murmured the clerk.

"Bet very special price, too," whispered Steven into Trish's ear.

"Maybe not, Steven. Ask him."

"What is your asking price of this one? The one my wife is holding."

"Very special price. Because of history, it's only $10,000 US."

"Tell me more; what is its weight?"

"It is," and the clerk referred to the slip of paper in the tray. "60 carats and very high quality; clear; and excellent cut and polishing."

"What is this history you speak of?" asked Steven.

"I would rather not say at this time."

"How so?"

"It might influence you if you or your wife are superstitious. It is a special one-of-a-kind stone not to be overlooked."

"Steven, it has such a unusual feel to it as it warms my hand, and I am not superstitious."

"Okay but $10 grand is a bundle; and if it turns out to be a fake back home, you are going to have to work hard to make it up to me."

"Could that be in the bedroom?" smiled Trish.

"It doesn't have to be a fake for that, you kidder."

"Keep it low, Steven. This little man speaks English."

"Sir, would you consider $5000 cash in US dollars?"

"The price is set by the owners, but for cash, let me check with my superiors."

The clerk exited through the beaded door as Trish whispered to Steven "What are you doing? That is all the cash we have for the entire trip."

A few short minutes later the clerk slipped through the beaded curtain with a catlike smile on his face.

"That will be most satisfactory. Please follow me." Seated in a room aside with a desk-like table and overstuffed mauve velvet swivel chairs and soft lighting, the sale was completed.

Back at the hotel, Trish held the velvet box that contained the large heart-shaped sapphire and commented to Steven "You should not have had that much money on your person. What a risk, but I am overjoyed you did. I don't recall ever seeing a picture of a sapphire cut like a heart. I wonder what the history is that he would not tell us? At least he gave us the name and city of the previous owner. That is not a lot to go on, do you think? We can search for him on the Internet and hope we come up with some leads. We have had a wonderful visit here but now, with that gorgeous sapphire warming my hand, I feel the trip is over for me. I'm satisfied. I am ready to go home and see the babies."

"You will have to hang in there a couple of more days, Trish. The Star Ferry is fun, and the view from the top of Hong Kong Island is not to be missed. Anyway, your Mama is in hog heaven with those babies. I never saw a woman go to such lengths for her grandchildren who were only going to be at her house for ten days. You'd have thought she was taking custody! New bed for the baby, dressing table, low toddler bed for Adam. It would have been a better choice to have her come to our house."

"Now Steven, you know that wouldn't work. She wants to show them off to her friends and at her church," Trish said. "Mom sure was pleased as punch none of her friends ever kept grandbabies that young for ten days. Remember, Amy is only ten months old."

"How are you doing? Missing her?"

"No major problem. She is weaned, and she adores Mama, but I must admit I feel a little different. I am what is known as an older mother in some circles — 44 and with two babies. Most of my friends from high school and college have children in their twenties. I had a late start. But boy, am I glad I did."

Trish smiled and winked at Steven. Her mom probably missed them all these miles away but understood they wanted to take advantage of being in Hong Kong and seeing the sights.

"Glad you feel that way, Trish, 'cause there was no way I was going to leave and then return any sooner considering the cost and miss all the sights. It will be a long time before we come to Hong Kong again."

Steven hung up the phone. "It's good to stay in touch with your mom and your friends, and I know that your expensive totem stone should make up for us staying another few days."

"Totem stone?"

"It must be. Your instant connection and the warmth and tingle you get from it. I didn't feel anything when I held it. In fact, it felt cool not warm. I admit I am curious and mystified as to what its history is."

"You realize we'll have to pay some duty on it?"

"Sure, Trish. I'd never try to sneak something back to the states. Even if I got away with it, my conscious would eat me up with guilt. I couldn't enjoy it."

"You sound like some of my Catholic friends with the feeling guilty bit."

"Trish, other people than Catholics feel guilty about doing things. We Methodists know a thing or two about feeling guilt. In this case, it would be stealing by not paying the duty. Like a person wearing a different colored shirt. It's still the same person just a different shirt. Same thing. It's stealing, just a different form."

"Steven, would you feel less guilty if the cost were less?"

"No, it's just the principle of the thing."

FIVE

"Hi, it's me." It was two weeks later when Trish phoned Barb.

"Good to hear your voice, Trish."

Barb Bonno, a forensic toxicologist and one of Trish's closest friends, had low back problems. Trish told her it was her repressed anger, but Barb, a thinker, didn't buy that line yet, as her mother suffered the same until her surgery for spinal stenosis.

"What's cooking around school?" asked Trish.

Barb Bonno possessed a spider web network of contacts in the Medical Center as well as across the country.

"Mostly the same. As you know, Parker is off on another of his trips, but I do think he has a couple of new faculty signed up. So, with the new guys on board, think you'll stay a while longer? I haven't whispered a word, not even to Clare, about your possible retirement."

"Thanks, Barb, I appreciate that. It's going to be hard enough if I do decide to leave. I need to see how much I have in retirement funds. Of course, I can't touch that for twenty years or so, but Steven has been most supportive."

"Trish, you're tenured. You could coast if research funds dry up, but I know you couldn't tolerate that."

"You're right about that."

"Anything new on the Biochem fellow's death?"

"Nope, not that I have heard."

"You think something is fishy?"

"Not for sure, though I do have a tickle at the base of my

brain. Got to run, and Barb, keep in touch, and keep your ear to the ground. Catch you later."

❀

SIX

It was two weeks later and although it wasn't full summer, the Saturday morning gave hint of a hot humid day, the kind that produced a subtropical afternoon shower. Steven took Amy, his and Trish's ten-month-old daughter, with him to his office. Although the office was not open, he wanted to check on a couple of things, and Trish wasn't too keen on Amy being at the beach even in the morning, sunscreen or not. With the sun in mind, mornings were best for their two-year-old son, Adam, and a return home by ten-thirty or eleven at the latest worked well. The Mississippi coast beaches, although not the sugary white of north Florida, were adequate for a two-year-old who thought he was four. With the barrier islands, the water did not deepen to waist deep until fifty or sixty yards from shore.

"What color will it be today, Sport? Green or purple?"

The sunscreen came in colors, and Trish was careful to slather it on his fair, little, baby-boy body.

"Green," said Adam, pointing to that tube. He didn't know his colors yet, but Trish pretended he did.

"Okay, so you'll be a green monster."

"Green munster," chirped Adam, wiggling and anxious to get to the gently lapping grayish water. No clear green water here, but it was satisfactory and close to home.

"Here, you've forgotten your hat." Trish placed the over-sized red, white, and blue striped hat decorated with stars on his head and adjusted the elastic under his neck.

"Now, you wait until Mama puts her sunscreen on."

Trish sat on the old bedspread she used for a beach blanket and with care applied SP-40 over her long legs and everywhere she could reach. At forty, she had a late realization of the need and became a more zealous user of sunscreen. Adam played happily at the edge of the beach, digging in the sand with his little plastic shovel, filling his small bucket and promptly turning it over.

"Okay, all ready. Let's walk down to the water."

Adam led the way into the water up to his knees at which point he sat down and splashed his hands. He got up and ran back to Trish who sat at the water line, her large Panama straw hat shading her face.

At this hour, few folk graced the beach, now clean from the sweepers, awaiting the daily deluge of debris that appeared like mushrooms sprouting from damp leaf mold on a forest floor. Only this was a sand beach and the mushrooms were paper wrappers, beer cans, paper sacks, discarded condoms, and plastic pop containers.

"Adam, I wonder if everyone who comes to this beach is illiterate. There are signs everywhere saying *Don't litter. Fine if caught.* Do you think they catch anyone? I suppose we can bring Amy next time. After all, the sun isn't as fierce as I thought this time of day, and with plenty of sunscreen, she'll be okay."

Trish, half lounging in the gentle waves at the water line, propped herself up on her elbows.

"Don't go too far, Adam. Come over here; let's make a sandcastle. Look, watch Mama," said Trish, pouring a slurry of sand and water to create tiny stalagmites of sand, delicate and growing with each handful. Trish loved this activity since childhood, allowing the water to wash over her as a primitive ritual. The sand was better over on Dauphin Island, Orange Beach in Alabama, or even out on Ship Island, but Trish didn't have the time to go that far for a few hours. Little Adam didn't know the difference. He was happy as a clam where he was.

Aware her crotch was filled with sand; she sat up and continued to build the sandcastle thinking that later in the summer, the family would go to the fishing camp on Bon Secour River. There, it would be a short drive to the Alabama beaches, and Steven would be along to help with the kids. In her heart, she considered this place a poor excuse for a beach, but kept her thoughts to herself so as not to be perceived a complainer.

God forbid you complain about sand in the crotch or a less-than-pristine beach.

The sandcastle was taking on a life of its own and, she judged, one of her best.

"Come here, Adam, and help me build our sandcastle."

The toddler squatted on flat feet with green knees bent as he knocked over the towers Trish had constructed and laughed.

"No! Help Mama; don't knock it over. Fill your bucket with water. Here, let me show you. You play with your car."

Trish pulled a plastic dump truck from the beach bag, which Adam found more entertaining. She resumed her building, humming under her breath and then said, "This kind of castle is how I imagine Cinderella's. Lots of people make sandcastles, packing the sand into buckets and then turning out the sand. That's okay, but I like these delicate forms you get dropping dribbles of sand and water."

She loved the time at the beach, even thought scant in shells, clear water, or surf. When surf was wanted, it was a short hop to Ship Island; however, the first boat didn't leave as early as she'd have wished.

"I'll tell you what, Adam. We'll go over to Ship Island before we go to Alabama. I promise."

Adam could care less, and Trish knew the trip was more for her and it would require more effort to keep him under control. Self-absorbed in her daydreams and the sandcastle, she looked up to see he had wandered away.

"Damn! And I thought I was watching him" she said

under her breath as she rose to collect him a scant ten yards away.

She was a slender woman who belied her chronological age and was careful about her health. She ate a good diet and exercised at the gym three times a week. Most guessed she was closer to thirty-five than the true, fast approaching forty-five. *Tan and fit* best described the woman in the floral Speedo swimsuit as she chased the toddler who ran laughing, "Catch me, Mama."

As she scooped up the toddler, her gaze shifted down the beach where two deputy sheriffs stood at the water's edge, hands over their brows against the water's glare staring at a dark shadow a few yards out in the shallow water.

The dark shadow on the tan gray water of the Gulf caught her eye as well. Curious, Trish waded into the water a few yards to get a better look and then she realized what it was.

"Holy shit! Is that what I think it is?" she whispered.

Then Adam saw the shadow.

"What dat, Mama?"

"Nothing, sweet."

"Better move back, Ma'am. Looks like a body there. Wouldn't want to scare the little boy," shouted the fat deputy.

Trish turned and retreated with great splashes to her spot on the beach.

"Time to go home now, Adam."

As she snatched the old bedspread, turning her back to the water, hoping Adam would not see anymore, he squirmed free. She didn't notice one of the officers approached as she had her head down and was mumbling to herself as she searched for her car keys.

"Back to your Mama, little man." The officer took Adam by the hand and returned him to Trish.

"God, there's so much in here. Okay, here it is. Shit, I didn't need to do that. Here is a policeman anyway," she said, looking up with a startled expression.

"Officer, thanks. He got away from me. Is that what I think it is?"

"Afraid so, Ma'am. How long have you been here?"

She took the toddler's hand and sat him on the ground and slipped her white mesh beach dress over her head.

"Since about ten, deputy."

"Stay, Adam, stay," she said, fearful he would run again.

"What dat?" asked Adam, again pointing to what appeared to be a claw-like hand protruding above the water.

"Only a piece of wood. This nice policeman is taking care of it."

That hand looked as if crabs have given a work-over. Just my luck. Now I'll have to talk to the police.

"Can we continue this by my car, officer? I can control this child better there."

"Sure thing. We have a couple more men on the way."

Trish draped the spread over her shoulder, taking the large straw beach bag in one hand and the toddler in the other, first seeking to distract him with a box of juice.

"Here, juice with a straw."

"What dat, Mama?"

"Nothing, just an old piece of wood."

With few people on the beach, she had lowered the windows and with the breeze it was not unpleasant inside. With Adam safe in his car seat, she stowed the beach bag and bedspread and turned to the officer who stood beside the vehicle waiting for her.

This deputy, a tall rangy, white man with a handlebar mustache curled slightly on the ends, tipped his hat and smiled at her.

"I hope that scene down on the beach didn't upset you or the little one."

"Officer, may I take him home now? We have had enough beach for this day."

"This won't take long. What's your name Ma'am?"

"Trish McLeod. Doctor McLeod." Then she thought, *I wish I hadn't said I was a doctor.*

"Oh, a doctor. Do you want to take a closer look? I'll watch your little boy. The Coroner's Office will be here in twenty minutes or so to fetch the body."

"No thanks. I've seen enough and I have my son here. May we go?"

"Okay, give me your phone number and someone will contact you for a more detailed account of what you saw."

"Thanks, officer. Glad to help anyway I can. Okay, Champ. Home we go."

❁

As she entered the kitchen, Mercedes, standing at the sink rinsing crowder peas said, "Thought I would shell these and get them on before I go home."

"Thanks. Would you change Adam's clothes for me while I shower? We had an exciting day, but a terrible thing happened. Let me get the sand out of my body and I'll tell you all about it."

"Sure thing, Dr. Trish. Come on, Mr. Toot. Did you have a good time at the beach? Your sister's taking her morning nap."

"I make sandcastle," chirped Adam.

"Great. One of these days, I'll go to the beach and see your castle. Let's get that green stuff off of you and you into some clean clothes. Need to potty?"

"Nope."

"I bet you did it in the water at the beach."

Adam averted his gaze.

"Sure as tooting you did."

Trish left the spread on the floor by the washer and put the beach bag on the dryer with her sandals. *The less sand, the better,* she thought as she headed for a shower. *No, I think I need the bath.*

"One of my favorite parts of the house," she mused, stripping her swimsuit while the water flowed into the tub. She decided to do a bubble bath, taking advantage of Mercedes' presence. Her garden bath was an oasis, and the grouping of green, closet plants around the deep, large Jacuzzi tub gave the illusion of a pool in a tropical jungle. Then the thought of a jungle brought snakes to her mind. The last thing she wanted to think about in the tub was snakes or other creepy animals.

She checked the digital clock as she sank into the plumeria-scented bubbles, so as not to overstay her allotted ten minutes. She had, for the most part, followed the suggestion of her dermatologist, but today she needed something more. *Hot and long; say fifteen minutes*, was the ticket.

Twenty minutes passed and Trish flipped the drain release with her toe.

She slipped into her Saturday-at-home clothes — denim shorts, tee shirt and flip-flops. With Trish, Wal-Mart clothes were Saturday clothes. "No need to have baby puke on good clothes," she thought.

Mercedes was watching Adam play as Trish entered the den and she asked, "What's this that happened at the beach? Adam's been saying 'policeman and piece of wood.'"

"Just a minute. Let me get a V-8 from the fridge. There's not much to tell." Adam played happily with two trucks at their feet.

"Is it okay to tell with him here?"

"We didn't see much detail — a hand that appeared crab-bitten."

"Lordy me! Was there a body attached? Think it was there all night?"

"Can't say how long, but the other part of your question is 'Yes.' The water's so shallow, and I didn't smell anything, but then we were at least ten yards away. And there were two cops, actually deputies, looking at it when I noticed them. It grossed me out. Reminded me of why I went into psychiatry.

Adam was in the water just a few minutes earlier. I wonder how far contamination from a body would spread. Did you bath him good? Did you look at the morning paper?"

Mercedes nodded.

"So, no missing persons reported?"

Mercedes nodded again and said, "Dat don't mean nothing 'round here."

"I expect I'll have a visit from the police soon. I thought Steven had the baby?"

"Oh, Mr. Steven, he called 'bout the time you all left. Said could I come for a while 'til you get home. He wanted to go fishing over at Deer Island. Heard from a buddy that the speckled trout were biting, so, as I didn't have much going on at my house and knew you'd be back soon, I came on over. I'll put the peas on to cook for ya'll. What you want in them, your usual? Now, your mama said she always had a little salt pork or slice of bacon. You being all health like, as things is changed, want canned chicken broth and three drops of liquid smoke. But, I do have to admit, Dr. Trish, this way is mighty tasty and little Adam, he shore do like Crowder peas; the baby do too, for that matter. I be moseying along if that's okay with you?"

"No problem, Mercedes. Things are under control. See you Monday morning."

It was lunchtime when Steven returned home. Trish, feeding the baby in the high chair and Adam eating chicken nuggets and crowder peas one at a time, were a happy group in the kitchen.

"What's cooking, babe?" asked Steven as he kissed his wife on the back of her neck.

"Crowder peas. Catch any fish?"

"Nice mess of trout, but they weren't biting as well as Chip said on the phone and that's usually the case, isn't it?"

"Steven, you'll never believe what we saw at the beach."

"Clue me in?"

"A body in the water.

"No kidding?"

"No, I'm serious. It was really gross. Adam had run away and I looked over and saw two deputies looking at a dark shadow in the water. Adam said 'What dat?' and when I looked closer, I saw what looked like a hand above the water. I think the crabs had gotten to it. The deputy yelled not to come closer and walked over to where we were. We got out of there pronto. I didn't want Adam seeing anything gross, and neither did I. We were about ten yards away. Think the water was contaminated where we were?"

"Not any more than usual."

"I had Mercedes bathe Adam good, and I did the same."

Adam banged his spoon on the table, "Daddy, we see big piece of wood."

"That's what I told him it was. I don't think he saw anything in detail."

"Have a good time, Buddy? Did you build a sandcastle?"

"Sandcastle," replied Adam.

"When you're a big boy, say five years old, Daddy will take you fishing. Here, let me wipe your hands, get you in some clean pull-ups, and it's nap time for you and baby sister."

Trish barely had Amy in bed when Skip, her golden pound puppy, gave a soft woof. "That dog has the keenest ears," said Trish as she peered out the window to see a police car out front. Quickly, she opened the front door before the officer could ring the bell.

"Hi. Wanted to keep you from ringing the bell. It drives the dog crazy, and the kids are down for a nap. Come on in, officers."

"Thank you, ma'am. Are you Dr. McLeod that talked to the deputies down on the beach this morning near the body they found?"

"Yes I am, officer. It was horrid."

"Did you recognize the person?"

"No, I didn't get closer than ten yards. I have nothing much to offer."

"What time did you get to the beach?"

"It must have been a little after ten. I built my little boy a sandcastle."

"So that was your handiwork we saw? Nice sandcastle."

"Thanks, Officer, that was my second effort. Adam knocked the first one over. What do you guys know so far?"

"As you probably noticed even from a distance, the crabs had been at work, so he was in the water overnight at least. At this point, he appears to be an Asian male, mid-to-late thirties. No shirt, but black cotton trousers. Had a tattoo behind his ear, a blue heart. I've seen a few tattoos in my time, but nothing like this one. It was the only mark on him except for a couple of scars; appeared fairly well nourished."

"Did you see any wounds?"

"To tell the truth, I didn't do a complete inspection or turn him over. When we get the autopsy report from the Coroner's Office, we'll know more then. All I saw was the tattoo and the healed scars, which were not anything to call home about."

Trish felt a chill run up her spine. "A blue heart?"

"Yes, ma'am. That familiar to you?"

"No, nothing, just that it's unusual. I thought when someone had a heart tattoo, it was red."

"Me, too. The ones I've seen were always red. Maybe this is the Chinese way."

"Would you happen to have the name of any of the detectives who will be working this case?"

"I think it will be Bill Swanson. Since the body was found inside the city limits, the police will handle the case rather than the Sheriff's Office."

Trish remembered that Bill Swanson was the guy her policeman friend, Clyde, had no use for, and he also was the officer who had questioned her about the dead Biochem fellow at her office. In spite of his big ego, she admitted he was a pretty good detective. He could even be a better cop if he weren't quite so high and mighty.

"I won't be seeing you anymore, ma'am. Detective Swanson will take over the case on Monday; he's on leave and due back in town tomorrow. If he needs to, he'll contact you."

"Of course, anything I can do to help. Let me know."

As she escorted the polite deputy out the door, Trish's mind wandered back to the beach scene. *Boy, that scene at the beach reinforced why I didn't consider pathology as a specialty. At least it was early in the day, and the odor was not apparent. Yep, one thing I can't tolerate is the sickening aroma of a corpse, fresh or ripe, even the embalmed cadavers.*

Vexed at the unwelcome memories of Medical School and clinical-path conferences to determine the cause of death, she was relieved to have found an option to track causes in the mental arena. In a way, it was sleuthing as much as police tracking down a killer. She followed a trail of crumbs the patients left to the source of his or her mental distress. Sometimes, she found the trail, and sometimes, the birds — so to speak — ate the crumbs as she wandered around the forest of the patient's psyche. It was win a few, lose a few. That was the way with psychotherapy as well as solving murder cases.

At this point, it was not certain the Asian man on the beach with the blue heart tattoo had been murdered. Drowning was a possibility after a fall from a fishing boat. The coroner would give a cause of death, and McInnis was a sharp as they came. Not much got by him. Even pathologists in Mobile and New Orleans consulted him.

If he fell from a boat and drowned, someone would have reported him missing. Maybe they did, but I don't know that. I'll have to reconnect with my policeman buddy, Clyde. He still does off-duty security work for the Mental Health Clinic. He was and is a terrific source of information as long as he keeps Bill Swanson from knowing his interest.

She hoped she wasn't going to become involved in the poor man's death as she had when she observed Hilda Rasberry's bloody corpse in the bathtub at the Mental Health Clinic. Trish rationalized, *That was different.* On that case, fellow faculty members, Clare and Barb, as well as her old high school friend Helen, now the catering queen of the coast, helped out.

She believed she had done her duty, yet in her mind she was unsure, as the wheels of curiosity were grinding once more. *Can I help it if I am curious? It won't hurt to ask Clyde what's been discovered.*

As Trish moved about the family room picking up toys, she whispered out loud, "I wonder if there's any connection between a blue heart tattoo and my sapphire. It came from Hong Kong and is the same shape, and the little man that sold it had a blue heart tattoo on his hand. Could it be a group symbol indicating membership in a society or clan?"

Trish probed under and behind the overstuffed cushions of the den sofa in a vain effort to locate Adam's missing sneaker with Pooh Bear on the toe.

That boy, he's forever hiding things. I hope he isn't going to have AD/HD. Don't go off on that tangent. He's a healthy, active two-year-old boy. What do I expect?

On her knees, butt in the air, she fished the hidden shoe from under the sofa as Steven walked in the room.

"Interesting position you have there — rather inviting."

"Oh, you," she smiled.

"Kids still asleep?"

"Yes, both of them should be for another hour."

He pulled her to her feet and into an embrace kissing her on the neck. "Want to make out? We have an hour."

"Maybe. Is the garage door closed?"

"Yes. Why?"

"So anyone dropping by might think we're not at home."

"Are you expecting anyone?"

"No, are you?"

"Only expecting a little fun with you"

Trish smiled at him as she closed the drapes in the den and padded after him into their bedroom, cool and inviting, the ceiling fan humming a lazy arc. As she closed and locked the door not to emerge for the next hour, she began to hum *Love Is a Many Splendored Thing* under her breath.

The wailing of the baby penetrated the door as well as screeching from the monitor.

"A little nap after good lovemaking is always a pleasant thing," said Trish as she arose.

It was precisely two hours after Amy's nap began.

"Up and at 'em."

She heard Steven singing in the shower. "Oh, the ocean waves may roar…." It was his favorite sea chantey.

It was a miracle the phone hadn't rung for three hours, a record for their house.

As she finished changing the baby, Adam toddled from his room.

"Where Daddy?"

"He's taking a shower. He'll play with you in a minute."

Baby on her hip, Trish headed for the kitchen to start supper. Adam followed, a Hot Wheels car in each hand.

"Cookie?"

"Sure thing, Champ, but only one. Put the cars down."

She fished a Graham cracker from the box with one hand after Amy was secure in her swing.

"Here you go. One for each hand."

Adam thought the crackers were cookies and so Trish called them that also, as she thought they were a little healthier. Steven and she preferred healthy food and expected their kids to follow their example. Steven came into the kitchen and fished a Diet Dr. Pepper from the fridge.

"Drink?" said Adam.

"A little milk in your sippy cup because supper is soon."

"Play with him awhile, will you, Steven, while I get supper on?"

As she removed a package of ground turkey from the freezer, the phone rang. Hooking the phone against her ear, Trish continued her preparations and answered. "Hi, mama. Fine. The kids are up from a nice two-plus hour nap, and I'm working on supper. Ground meat, spaghetti sauce. No, I'm making it from scratch; I use only canned during the week, or if I am in a hurry. Oh, maybe."

At that moment Steven entered the kitchen and proceeded to sniff the air.

"Steven, do I have an invitation to sail tomorrow afternoon with you and the fellows? This is mama. She wants to know if we would like her to babysit."

"Accept. Don't turn down any freebies."

As she stirred in the sauce, Trish continued. "Mama, he said "Great." What's Daddy doing? That's right, he's back into golf. It's not too hot for him to play in the afternoon? Hope there's a breeze. About tomorrow: we'll be back from church by 12:20, so come on over, say one-ish. Yes, we did see a body. How did you know? No, I don't think it will have any effect on Adam. He didn't see much. I told him it was a piece of wood."

"I am telling you, Trish, the Coast is a small town in many ways. Every body knows everyone else's business. Old Mr. Busby," she continued, "who lives down the highway, saw your Ford and the police cars at the beach and picked up the word from the police scanner in his truck, and he called your Daddy."

"No, I don't know who he was, mama. Maybe it was a fisherman."

"Okay. But, Trish, don't get nosey. Bye now. Love you."

"Love you too, mama."

Trish wondered why she went through that ritual, but her mother insisted and 'bye now' wouldn't do.

"How's spaghetti, broccoli with cheese sauce, crowder peas, and salad sound, Steven?"

"Great. Any dessert?"

"If you're a good fellow, I may liberate some of mama's pound cake from the freezer."

"Sounds like a winner."

Little Adam would eat spaghetti and anything with

cheese on it, so this was a winner dinner and another step toward total table food.

❀

SEVEN

The next morning, Steven backed the Land Rover out of the garage.

"It's another world getting to church with two kids," said Trish. "I never thought much about it, but this is an African safari in the making. At least we can afford car seats for both vehicles. Do you think in another year, when Adam is three, we will be leaving earlier to get him to Sunday School?"

"Trish, I'll take that challenge when the time comes."

"I'm thankful our kids don't make a fuss about the nursery at church. One Sunday recently, I overheard the workers saying there were two little ones who never stopped crying. Nothing would console them. One like that can ruin a morning, but two? That's one job I will never volunteer for. I noticed a request for a childcare volunteer in the church newsletter. Not my cup of tea. I have all I can handle with our two."

"I expect you'll be forgiven. There will be time for that when you are old and gray." He winked at her.

"What do you mean by that, Mr. Smarty?"

"Take it anyway you like, Trish."

In the parking lot after church, Agnes Scott, a rather prim seventy-year-old that happened to be a deaconess stopped Trish to ask, "Didn't I read in the paper this morning you were a witness to that finding of a body down on the beach yesterday?"

"Yes, ma'am, but it was in the water, and I saw the deputies there. Adam and I were near by. I hadn't seen it before they brought my attention to it."

"Seems I remember you were the one who found Hilda Rasberry's body and that poor girl at the Medical School. What is it with you, always coming up on dead people?"

"Nothing special. Once I was being helpful, and yesterday I was taking Adam to the beach early before the sun got hot."

"You be careful, my dear, about where you go and who you help. Now you have those two precious little ones to think about."

As they closed the car doors, Trish said, "That woman has no tact. What a busybody. How did she ever get a leadership role anyway?"

"She is a fixture around here. Her family founded the church."

"Old bird. Wish she'd keep her opinions to herself."

EIGHT

As they came up the street, Steven commented, "Your mother is already here. Isn't that her car in the driveway?"

"Yes, indeed. Hope she hasn't been waiting long."

"Hello, darlings. Trish, dear, you'd do better with some hostas around on the side of your house. There isn't enough sun for those petunias."

"Yes, mama."

Under her breath she whispered to Steven "Why does she always pick like that?"

Steven whispered back, "Beats me. Ignore her, as we usually do, and in a few days she will forget she said it."

"Have you been waiting long?" asked Trish.

"No, we went to early church and your daddy headed to meet his golf buddies, so I came on over early. You two scoot on ahead for your sail. I can feed the kids and get them down for a nap."

Fifteen minutes later, Steven and Trish were on their way to the boat. There were times when Trish thought the boat was competition for her. When he was younger, Steven had sailed quite a bit, even ocean racing, with his first wife, who'd now been dead for five years. She had been struck down in her thirties by breast cancer. It had been a good marriage, and once his mourning was complete, Steven was ready to move on when Trish came into his life. They had been casual acquaintances since childhood, but their relationship led him to believe in the concept of soul mate. He whistled a cheerful tune as they toted their gear toward the thirty-foot sloop moored at the Ocean Springs Yacht Club. Chip and Brad, his regular crew, were dockside and greeted the couple.

"A good day for a sail. Where are we going?" asked Brad.

"Out west toward Ship Island sound okay? My mother-in-law is with the kids. We need to get back by dark. There are thundershowers possible late, so let's not push it."

Although the boat could handle a storm, it took the fun out of a leisurely sail.

"Heard on the radio they identified that guy you found yesterday, Dr. Trish," piped Chip.

"Who was he?" continued Brad.

"I didn't exactly find him, guys. I was at the beach with Adam and by the way, you turkeys can call me Trish. I'm not that much older than you." She grinned and smiled. "The radio said he was some Asian type from the Far East most likely. He had a green card in his wallet and was working for a shrimper out of Bayou la Batree," continued Chip.

"That's a ways from here," said Trish.

"They said on the radio maybe the body was dumped from a boat. No clues about that, but interesting thing was he had a bullet hole in the back of his head, so he was killed execution style."

"Wow, I missed that information Chip. I must have been listening to another station."

"So are you going to solve the crime, Trish?"

"No, I'm not, Brad. Let the authorities find the answers."

"But, Trish, you were the one who helped solve that murder a couple of years ago."

"That may be true, but that was a one-time thing, I hope. Anyway, I have other fish to fry."

"How are things at the Medical School these days after you found that poor woman? I heard about that," asked Chip.

Chip was a science teacher at a local high school. Earlier in life he had considered a career in medicine. However, when he married early and kids came, he left that dream behind and now some fifteen years later said he was happy he had. He was great with kids, both his own and his students. He had been voted favorite teacher more than once.

"I can't say much about that either. Not a lot has come out, but I may be able to see what the post showed. What about your school, Chip?"

"Trish, not as many kids seem interested in medical careers now. A few years back when the first generation of Viet Nam immigrants' kids came along, many went into medicine. Now, the stream has slowed. Still see kids interested, but now they are a more mixed ethnic group."

"Chip, ever see a blue heart tattoo on any of your kids or hear of a group that wears blue heart tattoo?"

"No. A weird idea; seen lots of tattoos on guys, and gals too, for that matter, but never a blue heart. Why?"

"Oh, just that guy they fished out yesterday had a blue heart tattoo. I wondered if it meant anything special."

"I don't see kids much since school is out, but I'll ask around. I doubt if our fourteen- year-old would know. He's a pretty straight kid, not into acid rock, more of a country and western boy," said Chip.

With sails set and a fresh breeze, the graceful boat moved at a brisk six knots and Trish went below to read a book. Twenty minutes later she was topside restless and somewhat bored with the book and the cabin. She stood in the open hatch and surveyed the sea in all directions.

"Well, I'll be damned! Steven, do you see what I do?" A black sailboat under full sail moving to the east had caught Trish's attention.

"Hand me the glasses, Trish."

"What do you think?" she said handing the glasses to Steven.

"Nothing, just an interesting black boat. Looks like a junk. They're from Hong Kong. Don't see many of them in these parts. It does have an interesting logo on a sail though." He handed the glasses to Trish. "Do you see what I do?"

Trish pulled the glasses to her eyes and looked toward the

black boat rapidly departing from view. "Wow! There's a big blue heart on one of the sails. It is that same skewed shape my sapphire is and the tattoos I seem to be running across. Never saw that before on a sail and the boat is moving fast. They must be running the engine. I can't make out the name though."

"Did it look anything like the blue tattoo on the body you found at the Medical Center?"

"Yes, Steven, that's what I just said. It did; a slightly modified heart, not quite the usual symmetrical valentine shape, a little more narrow and elongated."

"That boat is gone for now. Wonder where it is heading?"

"We won't find out today, Brad. Look, there is cloud building to the southwest," said Steven. "Let's bring her in. We'll beat any weather in that bank."

"Ready about."

"Hard a lee." The crew responded to Steven's orders, and they were on the way back to the slip, calm waters, and safety. *It was good,* Trish thought, *to be away from the phone for the afternoon.* Of course, Steven had a radio; and if there was an emergency with the kids, her mother knew how to contact them; but there would be no calls from the Medical Center as she wasn't on back-up call. That was not the case when on shore. Too many times, the faculty member on back-up call was not available, and the poor resident or the hospital operator just went down the list, desperate for a faculty member. Trish, more times than not, was called upon to put out the fire. "But, you're so good at it. You know the system and resources," was the frequent excuse.

Trish didn't want to hear that anymore.

✳

NINE

Trish pulled her green Ford into her spot in the parking garage at the Medical Center the next morning.

"I'm a creature of habit," she noted, and decided to park in an entirely different place the next day for fun if she found one in the shade outside the garage.

She despised having to sweat. One would think she adjusted to living on the humid Gulf Coast. It was the time of year to switch from pantyhose to sunless tanning cream. That helped a little. She wanted tan legs without sweat, and knew that she had good legs, or at least, Steven thought so. She had dark hair but her skin was fair.

"Morning. Good morning. Hi." Trish spoke to everyone she passed on the way into the building and most replied in like manner. This morning she headed for her office before stopping by Sheila's office. A pink sticky note on the door read, "Call me. Clare." There was a smiley face. Trish smiled to her self as she juggled purse, tote bag, and briefcase to open the door. The office smelled of spice and orange.

"That was a good idea to have a bowl of potpourri here, especially since I'm not too sure of the ventilation," she murmured under her breath.

Trish had opted for a larger office rather than a smaller one with a window the last time offices were available when one of the faculty members left. She opened the small fridge under the counter that ran along one wall of the sixteen-foot-square office placing the week's supply of soy drinks, V-8, and yogurt inside.

Computer booted, she remarked, "At least the network is up today." Things technical dragged behind the rest of the world at the school it seemed, and the local network was frequently on the fritz.

She scanned and deleted most of the twenty or so emails from over the weekend with one hand as she stashed her purse in the desk. With the other, she picked up the phone to call Clare.

"Hi, what's up?"

"Are we sleuthing again, Trish?"

"Not that I am aware of. What are you talking about?"

"Read in the paper you found another body."

"Oh, that. No, I'm not involved, thank you, and I didn't find it. I was nearby with Adam making a sandcastle."

"Don't be too sure you won't be sleuthing with that curious mind of yours."

"Look who's talking, Clare. You are just as curious as I am. By the way, how's that rowdy crew of yours?"

"Kids are all shipped out to North Carolina for camp, and we have the house to ourselves for a month."

"So, are you keeping score?"

"Trish, we've been married twenty years. It's not like we hop in the sack three times a day like you and ol' Steven do."

"You don't know that."

"I wouldn't put it past you two. Every time I see you all together, both of you are moon-eyed even after three years of marriage."

"So, to change the subject, what's the latest dirt around the Medical School you have heard, Clare?"

"A patient escaped from the unit over the weekend."

"How'd that happen? Boy, bet nursing was bent out of shape over that."

"It seems he walked out with relatives who were leaving after visiting hours. Later the mama called to say he was home with her. And you know, they were the ones who probably brought him to the hospital to start with; wanted him out of their hair for a while. I'm glad I don't have to deal with those problems. C-L is a piece of cake compared with the inpatient unit. And, also, Two-Boy, remember him?"

"That nice black psych aide? Yes."

"He twisted his knee when a patient had to be restrained. He'll be out for a week."

"Gee, that must have been something. He's built like a tank and experienced."

"The patient was psychotic and high on cocaine, PCP, and, God knows what else. The beat marches on. Be glad your clinical assignment is the Mental Health Clinic and Outpatient Clinic."

"Yep, that has its problems, also but at least I can always write a certificate on them and have the sheriff or police bring them to you guys."

"Not me, Trish. Remember, I'm C-L. Say, since we're unencumbered, so to speak with no kids, you and Steven want to come for dinner on the deck Saturday?"

"On the deck? How's the mosquito load at your place? Last time I was there after dark, I got eaten alive by those suckers from that slew behind your property. The stagnant water must generate them by the millions."

"Trish, we have a new deal, a mosquito catcher. It is marvelous. And that water isn't stagnant; it just doesn't move much."

"Okay, in that case, I'll check with Steven. Let you know by Wednesday, okay?"

As she replaced the phone and rotated the chair toward the door, Sheila popped her carrot top head in the door.

"Here's a few messages for you I took off the voice mail this morning. How you doing?"

"Great, Sheila, and you?"

"Okay. Listen, are you locking your office door when you're not around?"

"Most of the time, why?"

"Oh, there's been another rash of thefts lately, but it was

mostly where the person didn't lock their office or desk and then wandered off. Dr. Suzanne from Neuro came 'round the corner kinda quiet like to see one of the research techs just leaving her office. She wasn't sure, so didn't say anything. I've noticed at lunch more than a few walkers coming by. Word must be out that this hall is on the unofficial indoor track. They look like office workers but have on athletic shoes. Probably want to see where the body was found. Heard via the grapevine another one of our department has his tail in a twist."

"Who? Cerzenski?"

"Yep, he's in to see the boss. Seems he somehow 'lost' his university ID in the parking lot of some apartments known as a pick-up spot for crack."

"There is always something like that going on around this place so it really isn't news." "When you run with a drug crowd, no telling what will crawl out, Dr. Trish."

"Fortunately, I don't have to deal with him. He goes to clinic at a different day than I do. I think I will go get a cup of decaf coffee from Martha's pot, Sheila. Don't let the turkeys get you down while I am gone."

"You are a hoot, Dr. Trish."

Martha had a long printout in hand when Trish entered the office.

"Good morning Martha. What's that?"

"Oh, a printout of phone calls in the department. This Chairman, Dr. Parker, doesn't want a bunch of unnecessary phone calls and has me checking long distance ones. By the way, do you know someone in Sri Lanka?"

"Nope. More of the crazy stuff going on around here. Sheila says there have been some thefts from offices left open so maybe same people are making phone calls. I may have failed to lock my door a couple of times. I have enough to worry about. Since they are after hours, must be someone in housekeeping."

"Martha, there isn't a security camera in that hall. If a person had a key, he would probably never be questioned if he were wearing a white lab coat."

"But the access from the hospital is closed after hours, and without a pass card no one can come in, Dr. Trish."

"That's a fallacy. The way students, residents, and staff leave coats lying around, anyone who was serious could have a duplicate key made," said Trish.

"You ever come up here after hours or on the weekends?"

"A couple of times over the years, and let me tell you, Dr. Trish, this place gives me the creeps on the weekend. I keep my panic button in my hand." It was a small beeper-size security alarm system provided by the university to be used if staff felt themselves to be in an emergency.

"I hope that made you feel better, Martha, but I doubt security can respond to a call in two minutes as they say they can. Heck, they're stretched too thin. Once, when I left my key at home, I called them to open up at 7:45am and it took at least ten minutes before the guy showed up with a master key."

"I will be careful, Dr. Trish. Don't forget, we have a department faculty meeting today at noon in the main conference room."

"Wouldn't miss it for the world. Ha!"

Trish found Clare had arrived in her office.

"Oh, hi, Trish" said, Clare. "Do you have a needle and thread? The hem on this pant leg is out."

"Sure thing." Trish pulled out a small sewing kit and passed it to Clare. "Clare, someone has been using my phone after hours calling long distance to Sri Lanka."

"Sri Lanka? I'm not even sure where that is. Indian Ocean?"

"You got it, Clare."

"Maps and geography always a fascination for me, but are of no particular use in the practice of psychiatry, Trish."

"I am really pissed off that someone is coming in my office and doing that. I bet they didn't know a log was kept. I don't know what I can do except be extra careful to lock my door when I leave. You walked in just now when I was around in Martha's office."

"Makes me think so too, Trish. My office is open now. We all need not to leave temptation around."

"I better get to work, Clare. Save me a seat at the departmental faculty meeting to the side and at the opposite end of the table from Rah Rah Boy."

"Who?"

"Our illustrious Chairman. Reminds me of a leprechaun cheerleader."

Clare laughed. "Okay. See ya noonish."

As Clare closed the door, the phone rang. "Yes, Cookie, I'm faculty back-up for Psychopharm today. A new volunteer? Okay, I'll be around in a minute."

Volunteers for Clinical Pharmacology research projects required a complete physical by a licensed physician, and Trish did her share. Everyone in the smallish department of full-time psychiatrists rotated duty. After twenty years, she was quick and thorough even when she performed the physical examination. More so than most psychiatrists in private practice where physical examinations were farmed out to internists or general medicine folk, here psych residents or faculty did the duty. Some of the old-timers with analytic backgrounds even preached touching the patients was a big no-no. Said it contaminated the transference.

"Well, there is no psychotherapy here, so it is okay," said Trish to herself as she locked the door and left her office.

It was twenty minutes later in the Research Unit exam room when she said, "We're almost finished. I'm just going to check your reflexes, and that will complete the examination. This is an interesting little tattoo on the inside of your arm. Is it a little blue heart?"

"Yes, I did it for my husband. He asked me to do it." "Oh, did he say why?"

The pale Asian woman blushed slightly as she whispered,

"Don't tell, please? He like to kiss me there and asked if I would have a little blue heart there."

"Oh, okay. Different strokes…etc., you know."

"My husband, he has a little blue heart tattoo there also." *Oh my God! Another blue heart tattoo and her husband has one also.*

"Okay, that's all we need to do. Thank you for volunteering. I'll see you from time to time. Usually when you come in, you'll be seeing one of our technicians or a resident."

Why didn't we ask more? She is the second volunteer with that tattoo.

'Cause we didn't think it proper.

Proper? Since when do we always have to be proper?

Look, the little lady is entering a depression study. It's just not appropriate to go into any detail regarding hidden symbolism of a tattoo, okay?

It seems strange to me that the fellow found at the beach had a blue heart tattoo and now this woman does. They're both Asian. Did you notice that? And so was the Biochem fellow.

Yes, I did. It's in the mind databank.

You better hurry, or you'll be really late for the show.

Show?

Yeah, the faculty show with Dr. Parker, the cheerleader leprechaun, as premier act.

The large seminar room next door to the department head's office was nearly full as Trish slipped into the chair Clare saved her, just before Dr. Parker cleared his throat and began.

"He's wearing a new wig," Clare whispered.

"At least it looks better than the shaved head he used to wear, remember? Got to give him a little credit for going from shaved like a billiard ball to the thatched roof look."

Clare giggled under her breath, "Wonder if it's matching?"

"What? Matching what?"

"You know…matching pubic hair."

"Clare, you're a piece," and Trish snickered also.

The meeting started over money as usual.

Dr. Parker cleared his throat and began. "Collections are up somewhat; however, we are still having to use funds from our clinical research areas for travel and to make up what is taken from departmental funds for your supplement."

"Didn't we hear the same song from the last chairman?" Trish whispered behind her hand leaning toward Clare.

"Sure did, and the one before that. I wonder if this one is shifting account monies around like ol' Dennis did," answered Trish.

"Probably so. Remember the old saying, 'power corrupts,' and this is a little bit powerful."

"I'll bet this guy is more of a boozer than Dennis was," continued Trish.

"Did you notice at that last Drug Dinner at the University Club? He had three of what looked like double martinis. At least there was an olive in them," continued Clare ignoring a frown from her neighbor at the table.

"When did we start counting people's drinks?"

"We don't ordinarily, Trish, but, remember, he was talking loud and making off-color remarks to Sonja, the EEG technician from Neurology."

At this point, Dr. Gomez sitting next to Clare put his finger to his lips and frowned. Trish stuck her tongue out at him and continued whispering as Parker droned on, seeming not to notice.

"What was she doing there anyway?"

"I think she came with Bill Small from Neurology as his guest."

"She is stacked, Clare, and could give Dolly Parton some competition. This is a rather boring meeting, n'est-ce-pas?"

"Aren't they all? Trish, let's entertain ourselves."

"How?"

"Oh, today, let's go around the room and guess how many of the guys that are married have had extra marital affairs?"

"Clare, we did that at the last meeting. It was four you said."

"Okay, well, today let's guess how many are closet queens?"

"Now that is stupid, Clare. How about how many of the gals are lesbian?"

"Ple-e-ase! Trish. That doesn't count?"

"Why?"

"There are only four women total, and that is too few to play that game. Anyway, we're all hetero hen medics in this department."

"What is out next topic, Clare? This is going to last at least another fifteen minutes."

"Okay, back to the body on the beach."

"I'd rather not. It was gross. I even dreamed about it again last night."

"What about all the blue hearts showing up? One on the body at the beach, one on the postdoc from Biochemistry, one on the sail of that Hong Kong junk, the two on the research volunteers, and you have a blue heart sapphire from Hong Kong in your silver drawer. And they are all that skewed shape. That is too weird."

"I have no idea, Clare. No one would believe this in a million years. It could it be the Asian equivalent of that smiley face you see everywhere. We certainly have quite a growing population of Asians on the coast. And by the way, my stone isn't in the silver drawer. Not anymore. I moved it, remember?"

"Oh, yes. I think that was stupid to put it in the freezer. A real thief would look there if he were really searching."

"Okay, point taken. I'll get Steven to put it in the safety box at the bank. Look Clare, I have this tickle at the base of my brain. We need to do some research on blue hearts — tattoos and otherwise."

"Now it's we is it? How are we going to do that?"

"Beats me, Clare, but we'll come up with something soon.

Tomorrow, I'll tell Clyde about them when I go to the Mental Health Clinic."

"What was that he just said, Trish?"

"Who? Parker the cheerleader? —oh—the next meeting he wants only the Steering Committee," Trish replied.

"That leaves us out. You're not the director of anything at present are you Trish?"

"No."

"Isn't that interesting?"

"Look, Clare, I've worked almost twenty years to accomplish that."

"Yay for our team!" whispered Clare.

Back in her office, Trish locked her door, turned off the overhead light, leaving only the low green gleam of the banker's lamp for light. She unlocked her desk and pulled open the left lower drawer, reached to the very back of it and retrieved a small zippered vinyl pouch that could pass for a cosmetic bag and removed a female external vibrator.

Why are we doing this?

Our neck is a little tight. We can use this on muscles too.

You know that's not why!

We faked our orgasm last night didn't we?

Maybe a little. It's always good to have a little tension release. That meeting was tedious, and I need some relief now.

Okay, make it quick and don't make too much noise. Remember, these walls aren't that soundproof.

It was only a couple of minutes later that she replaced the vinyl pouch in the drawer.

That was quick. We didn't even take off our panties.

Look, stop complaining. It's not lovemaking; it's just a tension reliever.

Be sure we don't get addicted to the vibrator.

Not to worry. I'm addicted to Steven.

Get off this kick and to work.

Okay, okay! Let's write the grade comments for the last group of medical students who rotated through the mental health clinic.

The afternoon passed quickly without undue hassles. For once, the third-year resident, Grace, seemed to be getting a handle on the process rather than content when she came for supervision, and Sheila had the rough draft for an article for the Green Journal on involuntary movement disorders ready for review. Trish, gathering her things to leave at five, stopped to answer the ringing phone.

"Hi, Brian. Okay, good day." A fellow faculty member, he asked Trish to cover for him on the ER the next morning as he was entertaining a virus passing through his body and about to set up shop in his throat. Trish liked him, so she agreed to his request. "I can stop by and check with the resident before I go to the Mental Health Clinic, and there will be time to find someone else to cover the rest of the day."

Are we really going home now?

Sure, just let me stop by the break room for bottled water. That's one good thing about this Chairman; he does keep a supply of bottled water handy for everyone. Okay, we're out of here.

Trish hiked her purse over her shoulder and walked quickly toward the elevators.

Going to use the stairs today?

Nope, the stairwells are getting hot.

What about the blue heart tattoo on that second volunteer?

What about it?

We've seen three of those suckers now on women. Don't you think that's unusual?

Not yet, but I need to look into that. I didn't see the one on the body at the beach, was only told about it. Tattoos are more common in today's world. Back in medical school about the only people who had them were gang members, or anyone who had antisocial personality disorders. Now you even see them on cute sorority college girls.

But any blue hearts?

Not until now. Remember that patient in Medical School who had a tattoo on his penis? God that must have hurt.

Said 'LOVE' didn't it?

Sure thing, and we scored a few extra points for remembering that and including it in the write-up of the physical exam.

Are we going to get a tattoo?

No way! Don't you even suggest it.

Now there are temporary ones, so if you get a wild hair that we need one…I can't imagine why.

That will have to do.

Don't forget to stop by the grocery. We need milk and eggs.

Trish noted the fourth level of parking garage already clearing out at five-ten and thought the garage a real blessing. She did not care if it did cost fifty dollars a month.

I'll admit it keeps us out of any weather, but even now it's beginning to seem creepy—dim—I feel better with open sky.

Sky may not be so creepy, but can be hot or rainy.

So, we have choices to make. No big deal.

Anyway, you have our little panic button. Better check to see if it's still working.

Trish pressed the test button on the small clicker attached to her car keys to hear the cricket chirps from the loud speakers indicating that if the panic button was pressed, the sirens, loud enough to wake the dead, would sound and University Security would be on the scene in two minutes or less she hoped.

I doubt that, but there is some sense of security, so it's worth the two dollars a month.

"Hi, gang." Trish entered the house from the garage. Adam ran to her, throwing his arms around her legs, "Mama, mama," and smiling broadly, Mercedes emerged from the kitchen, purse in hand.

"Everything's fine. Supper is on the stove, meatloaf in the oven, and salad in the refrigerator. I need to get on my way. Mr. Steve, he's out back checking on his tomato plants."

"Thanks ever so, Mercedes. I don't think I could make it without you. See you tomorrow."

Just then, Steven entered from the patio with Skip, the

pound puppy, mostly golden retriever, happily wagging his tail.

"They're looking good. We should have tomato sandwiches for lunch until September and some to share. That fish emulsion fertilizer must be magic." Steve was an aficionado of tomato sandwiches, especially on Helen's multigrain homemade bread. The bread was part of why Helen developed such a successful catering business with Trish's encouragement. His first venture into gardening, six tomato plants, was beginning to look like something from Jack-and-the-Beanstalk. The plants now almost six feet tall were, loaded with green tomatoes, with a few beginning to turn red.

Later, sitting at the table with Adam in his booster seat and little Amy in the high chair munching on a Zwieback cracker, he said, "How was your day?"

"Okay. I still keep thinking about that poor fellow found at the beach Saturday. Oh, and guess what, Steven? I happened to do a physical on a research volunteer, and lo and behold, she had a little blue heart tattoo on her inner upper arm."

"So?"

"I know tattoos are more common now, but I asked Clare, and she said she hadn't seen or heard anyone mention blue heart tattoos; roses, red hearts, but not blue hearts."

"Probably just a coincidence."

"Maybe, but I have a tickle at the base of my brain over them. There are four people I know about with that same tattoo, and it was on the sail of that junk."

"Trish, let it go. Don't go reading something into this."

"I'm not. But it is curious, and it was the same shape as the blue sapphire you bought me in Hong Kong."

"As I said, don't go looking for zebras."

"I'll think about it. Want to split baths tonight, Steven?"

"Sure, which do you want?"

"I'll take the baby. Adam does better with you, and then I'll read him his story."

"Sounds like a winner. Here we go." She removed Amy from the highchair, toting her under her arm like a bag of flour.

"Come on, Princess, bath time."

It was 8:30; the bedtime ritual was complete, including the required stories. This week it was *"Pickles the Fire Cat"* for the fifth time. Both children were in bed without incident.

"At least they don't fight sleep like so many I hear about, Trish."

"They get that from me. When it's bedtime, I want to go to sleep. Now, I need to call Helen. She was such a help when our gal gang – the Lunch Bunch — of Barb, Clare and I were discovering how Hilda died."

Settled in an over-stuffed chair with a glass of iced tea at her elbow, Trish punched in Helen's number.

"Hi, how's tricks?"

"Oh, hi, Trish. Fine here."

"Listen, Helen, sorry I haven't called in awhile. You heard I saw the body at the beach Saturday?"

"Lordy, yes. Was it gross?

"Yes, to be sure. Very gross, but what I wanted to discuss with you is the blue heart tattoos I seem to be coming upon everywhere. Do you have time to talk now?"

"Now is a good time, Trish. My ever-loving spouse has gone to his AA meeting. I am so proud of him and his staying in recovery as he calls it. A blue heart tattoo, you said?"

"Yes, blue heart. He had a blue heart tattoo, and I have seen two research volunteers and the poor girl I found in the stairwell with the same shape tattoo. It isn't a regular heart-shape. More skewed the same shape of the sapphire Steven bought me in Hong Kong. I am beginning to feel nutty with the number of times I have run across that shape lately. Clare says she's never seen one like these either. Have you?"

"No, Trish," answered Helen as she continued painting her long fingernails a hot pink with the phone crooked on her shoulder.

"What about the girl you found at the Medical School? That must have been almost as bad as finding Hilda's body."

"It wasn't near as bad because there was no blood, Helen. I haven't heard anything more about her death. I'm going to the Mental Health Clinic tomorrow after I check by the ER at the school and I'll ask Clyde if he has any information."

Trish continued, "Are we on for lunch Friday?"

"Sure, Jacqueline's?"

"You got it. Make that 11:30, before the lunch bunch crunch invades the place. I'll see if Clare and or Barb can join us."

❋

TEN

"I'm here! Good morning." It was Mercedes; regular as clockwork at 7:00 a.m. Adam came out of his room rubbing his eyes.

"I hungry."

"Breakfast coming up, shore thing."

"Baby's still asleep," said Trish from her room.

"Mr. Steven gone already?"

"Yep, said he had a busy day. Thought he could leave early though. Okay, I'm out of here. Let me check with the resident on call from last night," said Trish grabbing the phone and pounding in the number.

"Hi, Dr. Trish here. Any leftover patients? Great! Dr. B called. He's ill so won't be in to check you out. Beep me if you need anything. Dr. Parker or one of his lackeys will get someone to cover for Dr. B the rest of the day. I'm on my way to the Mental Health Clinic." She applied her usual blue eye shadow as she spoke.

"Here's your lunch I fetched from the fridge for you. That's smart to fix it the night before," said Mercedes.

"Just another old habit of mine. Have a good day, Mercedes. Bye, Angel." She kissed Adam goodbye as he was happily eating Cheerios and milk.

Twenty minutes later, Trish pulled into a new spot in the parking lot at the clinic that would be in the shade until she departed for the Medical School after lunch.

"It does pay to be a little early. Most of the full time people screech in here right at eight o'clock."

"Getting a shady spot is a perk for being early, eh, Dr. Trish?"

It was Clyde, the off-duty policeman who had been such a help in the solving of Hilda Rasberry's murder.

"For sure. Hi, Clyde!"

"Morning, Dr. Trish."

"What're you doing outside the front door?"

"Nothing much; it's a nice morning. This duty can get a little boring some days sitting in that little office, so thought I would take a dose of fresh air."

"Say, if I have some no-shows, can you stop by my office for a chat?"

"Be my pleasure. I'll check with you in a little while."

Trish unlocked the door to the office she used.

Too bad I'm not am not here more often. This office is nicer than mine at the Medical School.

It wasn't only hers as other faculty from school used it on the other days.

It's large, and I like the plants. I can't have those in the Med School office with no windows. Maybe I should work on that again.

What?

An office with windows. Being tenured and senior should get us a few extra perks.

I'll put that on our list. Though that space was more important than a window at school.

Trish opened her soy protein smoothie, first shaking it vigorously. With the phone hooked on her shoulder, she punched in the receptionist line.

"Shanella, anybody here for me yet? Okay. Ring me if they show up."

Trish turned to the stack of charts, reviewing lab work for the social workers and initialing each to indicate an M.D. had noted the results. A few needed further attention. Most were within normal limits and not clinically significant. At that moment, a knock at the door diverted her attention.

"Come in. It's open."

"Busy, Dr. Trish?" asked Clyde, poking his head around the door.

It was Clyde in his navy uniform that strained over his stocky frame. With twinkling blue eyes and a profuse handlebar mustache, he was a perfect model of an Irish cop.

"No, first patient was a no-show, and the 9:30 called and canceled. Come on in and take a load off your mind, Clyde."

"Mind if I leave the door open in case anybody's looking for me?"

"Sure. Say, any news yet on that body from the beach over the weekend?"

"It's too early for the autopsy report, but word is he probably had the bullet in his head before ending up in the water."

"Did they get an ID on him for sure?"

"Yep. The green card in his pocket was valid. Some relatives are going to claim the body for burial or whatever. That's a little problem, because they're in Alabama — crossing state lines with a body and all."

"That shouldn't be a problem. The funeral home can arrange that. Look, Clyde, let me know what you hear about the post. I wouldn't be particularly interested, but he had that blue heart tattoo, and just yesterday I ran across another person with a blue heart tattoo. I wonder if there's any connection. This person, a woman, appears to be Asian also."

"Now, Dr. Trish, you aren't getting yourself involved in another murder case, are you? Wasn't that one a couple of years ago enough?"

"Don't get your panties in a knot. I am only wondering about the tattoo. And I did tell you the Asian girl in the stairwell at school had the same tattoo?"

"No, you didn't. Going to be here all day, Dr. Trish?"

"No, have to get back to school after lunch. Have a good day, Clyde."

"You, too, Dr. Trish. I'll let you know what I find out."

ELEVEN

It was a quick trip back to the Medical School, and for once, there was little in the way of traffic. Trish sat at her desk, rocking back and forth as she mulled over the recent events, especially the death of the postdoc fellow. *How did that girl get trapped in the stairwell?* The ring of the phone broke her train of thought.

"Do you have a minute, Trish?"

"Helen, of course. Good to hear your voice."

"Trish, do you think that girl you found was killed, or did she just collapse and die there?"

"Helen, I don't know much of anything at this point. I have this ongoing tickle at the base of my brain about this though. For now, I'm just sitting here. I can't seem to get my mind on work. I had a chat with Clyde. Remember how he helped on Hilda's case? He was at the Clinic this morning, and he is going to check on a few things. To switch gears, how's the sandwich business these days?"

"Trish, you know it is a full-fledged catering business, now and I have six employees."

"I was only teasing a bit. That's fabulous! I apologize for jumping around, but that's what my brain is doing these days. Back to the girl I found and that tattoo she had: perchance, do you have an employee who is Asian?"

"Why yes, Trish. I do."

"Great! Helen, would you ask her if she's ever heard of a group that identifies itself with a tattoo of a blue heart somewhere on their bodies? I realize that's a funny request, but at this point, I have no idea where to go with this."

"Are we reactivating our gal gang, the Lunch Bunch, and sleuthing again, Trish?"

"Maybe, Helen. Call me Miss Curious, for now. God, my mind is jumping like water on a hot griddle. How's that handsome hubby of yours these days?"

"Trish, he was doing so good with his recovery, but I am afraid he has slipped and is drinking again. Not a lot, but with his history *any* is too much."

"That's too bad. Are you sure he's drinking again? Maybe you could tell his AA sponsor. Do they approve of family, so to speak, reporting the lapses? Couldn't hurt. Don't enable. I know you've got that one down, Helen. Listen, we'll talk more at lunch on Friday. It will be great if all four of us can come."

"I should be able to come. Jacqueline's is it?"

"You got it. I'll get someone who owes me a favor to cover the students and we can all brainstorm and begin either to make a plan or let it rest."

Clare entered Trish's cozy but windowless office at the Medical School as she hung up the phone and took her feet off the credenza where she had propped them.

"Hi, Clare."

"Trish, are you going to the Aspen meeting this August?"

"I was thinking about it if Steven wants to go. He could do some trout fishing while I'm in morning lectures and meetings, and we could play in the afternoons."

"The way you guys play, all you need is a hotel room."

"Clare! Now, just because we have an active love life, doesn't mean we don't enjoy other activities. I thought we might take Adam if he's completely potty-trained by then. I just don't want to face taking Amy. She's just a toddler, and mama loves to take her up to her place and show her off to all her friends."

"If you're going, better get your travel request in right

away and get your coverage. I think some of the guys may take leave then, too."

"I'm past covering that inpatient unit; rank and seniority do have some privileges. The four Inpatient guys can cover each other."

"I don't know what it is, Trish, but August seems to bring out the manic patients in droves. Too many seem to think it's the time of year to go on a drug holiday and stop their lithium or valporic acid."

"Not only the folk with bipolar but for me, Clare, it started in late July and especially in years with an over abundance of rain. Remember that year we saw so many youngsters — kids, teenagers crazy as shit? It was the rain. A great crop of cycliban mushrooms grew out of cow paddies that summer, and the kids made a Kool-Aid drink with the mushrooms and experienced more than a few visual hallucinations."

"True. That was bad, Trish, but most of them recovered without permanent damage. Today we see a few every now and then over the top on PCP or when the marijuana joint has been dipped in embalming fluid. It's sad, but with the embalming fluid, that wipes out brain cells that never come back. Later those poor souls function like 80-year-old Alzheimer's patients. I wish there was something we could do for them."

"And Trish, remember, I want to see that sapphire Steven bought you in Hong Kong. Bring it to lunch Friday when we meet, will you?"

"Okay. Steven took it to Bourgeois, and they are mounting it so I can put it on a chain. I doubt it will be back by then; but if it is, I'll bring it. I do want you all to see it. It is very similar in shape to the tattoos I have seen lately. Oh, by the way, Helen is afraid Reg is hitting the bottle again. I wanted you to know before we have lunch Friday."

"I hope not, Trish. Is he still in the insurance business like Steven?"

"As far as I know. Helen didn't say otherwise."

"Steven know him?"

"It's a different agency, Clare. I don't think their paths cross that often."

"Let's pray for the best for Helen, Trish. I can't think of much else other than being a friendly ear that we can do. We can't see her for therapy, and I don't think she needs it anyway."

"I agree. By the way, Clare, are you going to the end-of-the-year party for the residents?"

"I haven't decided yet. Where's it to be this year?"

"At Parker's house."

"In that case, I'll put in an appearance and slip out as usual. You, Trish?"

"I'll be doing the same thing. This Chairman has been here only a little over a year, and I'm already getting bad vibes about him; and it's not only his excessive travel. A couple of the new people he brought are downright weird. At least we know they all had urine drug screens when they checked in. But, heck, if any of them are users, they are smart enough to abstain for a week or so. And that's mighty suspicious; I heard Cerzenski lost his ID card at a hot spot for drug deals."

"Trish, I heard that too, and earlier this year, I went to a drug dinner seminar given by Sandoz, and Parker, Cerzenski, and Spitz sat together and really put the alcohol away. I overheard them ordering double Martini's several times."

"Clare, I'm telling you, Parker is a lush. I don't care if he was a Rhodes Scholar and had five years at the Mausley. The biggest thing he got there was his fake British accent." "Let's keep our eyes open and ears peeled. I can tell you, I don't care how brilliant they are, a person passes from a heavy-user state to an abuse-state, and eventually the mistakes begin to show up; and it happens quicker with cocaine than alcohol."

"I agree, Trish. Alcohol is slower, and it may be ten or fifteen years after daily heavy use before a person begins to slip from what I have seen. Cocaine or amphetamines sooner, probably because their paranoia is more noticeable.

"Do any of our new weird ones, his lackeys, come up here to school, evenings or the weekends when not on call, Trish?"

"Ms. Gwen does. She's frequently the charge nurse on the three to eleven shift. She noticed Cerzenski on the unit of late — say 10:00 p.m. — and she had not seen him leave when she went home. She assumed he was back in the Faculty Office with the door closed. No telling what was going on in there. According to the staff here in the school, he never makes it in until 10:30 a.m. or 11:00 at the earliest, unless there's a meeting with the Dean or something called by hospital administration. Maybe he runs his day from eleven until nine in the evening."

"I don't think so for him."

"He is a funny duck, Trish."

"He seems suspicious to me. I have no reason to have a relationship with him, and I certainly don't have the authority to request a random urine drug screen. Since we all will be at the residents' party, that's a time to keep our eyes open. And if our chairman Parker is the lush I suspect he is, we'll see evidence there."

"Let's go to the department meeting, Trish."

It was another tedious meeting that droned on, same song, same boring verses. Sitting down, his russet hairpiece somewhat ruffled, Parker said, "We need to make more grant applications." Without any introduction or welcome, he tugged his usual yellow necktie and loosened it to reveal a hairy neck adorned with a thick gold chain.

"Hell," whispered Trish, "even if I had the time with all my clinical duties, when would I do the project if I did receive funds? I am not working more than 50 hours a week. That was necessary in the beginning of my career as part of going for tenure, but not now. I have kids and a husband. Anyway, I feel my calling, if you will, is more in the line of teaching than research."

The two women continued their aside conversation unnoticed by the men in the group.

"Where are we meeting for lunch on Friday?"

"I told Helen Jacqueline's."

"Great, they don't serve alcohol there, so it'll be a different group of customer to observe than we see at the usual watering holes."

"I'll check with Clyde for any information floating around about the blue heart tattoo guy and also the Biochem gal I found in the stairwell. That's pretty much a dead area in the building, not much foot traffic other than the walkers who pass by at lunch as I have commented on before."

"Trish, the detective who talked to me was that Bill Swanson. He questioned every one in this part of the building. He strikes me as a creep, a narcissistic creep. I remembered you talked to him when we were sleuthing Hilda's death. He hasn't mellowed a bit."

"Something will turn up sooner or later if her death was not a natural one. It always does. It's only that in real life. It's never as quick as in the movies."

TWELVE

Jacquelyn's, a cozy lunch spot, was located in a small antiques mall favored by local women about town. They and a few gamblers bored by the casinos kept the tables full most weekdays when reservations were necessary. In previous years before the antique mall when it was a neighborhood drugstore, teenagers frequented it for after-school sodas and fountain drinks. Helen arrived early and ordered cinnamon peach herbal iced tea and pulled out her crochet for a few minutes until Trish and Clare showed up. Ten minutes later, Trish and Clare slid breathless into their bent wood chairs.

"Hi, great to see you two. It's been too long since we've had lunch like this. Is Barb coming?" asked Helen.

"Not today. What are you making, Helen?"

"Oh, just some placemats. They make nice wedding gifts."

"Let me see," said Clare. "Boy, these are nice! What's the name of the pattern?"

"Queen Anne's Lace," piped in Trish. "I think my mama has a tablecloth her mother made in that pattern."

"You are correct. It's a popular pattern. It has been used around these parts for years and years. You two crochet?"

"I can whip out a fabulous chain I learned a million years ago in Girl Scouts, but that's it," quipped Clare as she opened the menu.

"I'm pretty much limited to potholders but," continued Trish "I have a great aunt who makes fabulous baby booties. She does them now for newborn layettes. Her church circle makes and donates them to the Medical Center for the babies of indigent mothers."

"It does keep the hands busy and once I have a pattern down, I can even watch TV."

"Can you read a book, too?"

"No, you joke. I can multitask, but that's an overload even for me. Must admit though, I did try it a few times. Enough of my little activities. What's going on in the exciting world of university psychiatry these days? Are we sleuthing again?"

"You mean the latest death?" asked Trish.

"Of course, and then, you saw that man dead on the beach. I hope little Adam isn't having nightmares about it."

"No, he's okay. We just happened to be near by. Adam hasn't even said anything about it since, and he did not actually see the body. But anyway, I think we'll go out to Ship Island next beach trip. There's a little more surf action. Of course, it wouldn't qualify as surf action in California, but it's more than the lapping along the highway beach." "Back to the Biochem fellow. Maybe hers was not a natural death," said Clare. "How is it three nice, regular gals like us end up discussing possible murder when we don't know how the poor girl died? And do we know what her name is yet?"

"It's Mi Ling. We don't go looking for it, and we do obey the law. I mean, we're upright, good citizens. It's our friend Trish here. She keeps coming across dead bodies. Three to my count! And look at me. I'm the same age. We were in high school together, and I've never come across a body — not even a bad car wreck! My only exposure to death is the occasional funeral home visit."

"Count yourself lucky, I certainly didn't go looking for death. In medicine, we deal with death on a regular basis, but not exactly this way. When I stumble across a dead body as I have with Hilda and Mi Ling, I do get curious as to what the facts are."

"And then she sucks me in, too," chimed in Clare as the waitress arrived to take their orders.

"Don't give me that! You both are as curious as I am. Look at you all, like cats waiting for cream. Okay, I did talk to Clyde last night; nothing much on the guy at the beach. His people sent a funeral home for the body and were going to have him cremated; something about taking his ashes back to Sri Lanka where he was from. He had been missing four or five days, but that wasn't out of the ordinary. He did that from time to time. His car was found in a roadside rest stop near the Alabama border. No sign of foul play, there, but I'm sure the investigators took some samples of dust, hair, whatever, for future analysis. The car went to the family and now a cousin is driving it." "What was his cause of death?" said Helen

"Clyde said it was most likely drowning even though he had a bullet in his brain because there was water in the lungs. He was near dead when the water entered his lungs any way."

"Maybe he was shot and then fell or was tossed off a boat?"

"But where's the boat? Or, if it were a large boat, why wasn't it reported?" said Clare.

"Clyde said no report of such, and if he was shot on a boat; they sure weren't going to report that."

"I believe you. Listen, I don't know much about tattoos, but I noticed a sign near PoBoy Express. It said Voodoo Tattoo Studio. I could stop by next week while on a sandwich run. One of my help asked if she could have a day off, so I will be driving that way. That is if you want to check further on blue heart tattoos." "That's great! If anyone would know about designs, they ought to."

"Also, I'll ask how long they have been open. I think not more than a couple of years."

"Say, pretend you're interested in having a tattoo yourself," said Clare.

"Oh, I don't know if I would go so far as to say that."

"Tell them your husband wants you to have one. Think up something kinky," said Trish.

"You shrinks, how weird!"

"She's just kidding. Don't take her seriously. Say, did I

hear right, you are getting a degree?" "Sure am. You know, I never did finish after Reggie and I married. I had two years of credits. It actually came about from the sandwich catering. I felt some business courses would be useful, and since things were calm at home with Junior in college and Reggie gone to his AA meetings two nights a week, the time opened up for me. It is going quite well. Should be finished in another year or so."

"Heck, why don't you just go ahead and take what you need to and finish? It's not like you have a forty-hour a week job to go to and, you lucky dog, you fell into good workers for your Philling Station catering business." "Oh, that. God just sent them my way. I prayed about it."

"Do you realize how trite that sounds at times?"

"Whatever do you mean? I was serious."

"Me, I'm not so sure it is that simple."

"Sure, the Bible says be like a little child. That's how a child would approach it."

"For sure sometimes, God love you, you act like a child. You could have finished school years ago. Junior wasn't born for a good many years after you married, as I remember," replied Clare.

"That's right. We had to get married and then I had that miscarriage. It was like God punished me for having relations with Reggie out of wedlock. In those days, I wasn't ready to buck Reggie. And now, I'm afraid he's drinking again."

"What makes you think that?" said Trish.

"Sometimes, I think I smell it on his breath. I have a sensitive nose and I can smell if he drinks."

"Could it possibly be something else?" said Clare.

"Hopefully so. He has been grouchy lately. Wants me to iron his undershirts like I used to. I told him it was the 21st century."

"Anybody tell you news of the cause of death for that Mi Ling you found?"

"Sheila will find out something for us whatever the cause

of her death was," said Trish "That woman has more contacts than an octopus has arms when it comes to gossip around the school. The Biochem Labs are a far piece from where I discovered the body."

"Did you ever see the Biochem gal in the hall or on an elevator?" asked Helen.

"No, but I'm not as observant as usual, I must admit, regarding postdoc fellows and grad students. Their white lab coats seem to blend together when I am in a hurry. Seems I notice medical students with their short jackets and green scrubs now as I teach them. In the past, they were about the only ones wearing scrubs but now, in, the past few years, the nursing staff has begun wearing scrubs. Each unit picks a color or print for either their unit or themselves. I like the change. Pediatrics has cute ones in a print, but surgery wears that toxic babypoop brown. I think that color was picked so there would be less likelihood of someone stealing them. When the same color was used throughout the institution, it was called surgical green. I saw guys in Wal-Mart wearing them and I'm certain they had no connection with the Medical School Surgery Department. Now, even the fat broads wear the scrub pants and not dresses, and I believe some of them have nothing to do with the medical field."

"An offshoot of women's lib," said Clare. "Back then, God forbid. If a woman wore scrub pants even in the OR she was labeled lesbian. Now, who cares anyway? But there still is a group that has white-coat-itis."

"What do you mean?"

"What she is saying is ever notice a gal, or even sometimes a guy, who is probably an orderly with a white lab coat at the supermarket or 7-11? There is no reason on God's green earth to do that. I think they feel it gives them prestige; maybe someone will think they are a nurse or doctor, rather than housekeeping or laundry workers. Remember when Ed Dandridge came as Chief of Surgery and implemented the rule of covering OR scrubs with a clean scrub gown when out of surgery? Took quite a while to get that accomplished. And even now, I see support staff walking all over the hospital with OR scrubs, but it's not for me to say anything." "Hell," said Clare, "I've said, 'Is that okay for you?' on more than one occasion, but not when a lot of people are around. Wouldn't want to embarrass some poor soul."

"When I think about it, I do see research lab tech types walking in from parking in their white coats and sometimes at the mall. But that's few and far between."

"Most docs do wear the white coat, carry it in the car and put it on when they arrive, but not wear it all over town."

"Of course, among us shrinks, the main staff who do wear a white coat are on the Inpatient Unit or doing research. I don't think I've ever seen a faculty person wear one at the Outpatient Clinic, or the Mental Health Clinic for that matter."

"The residents always wear theirs. It's a security blanket and, of course, we require the medical students to look professional. I have an occasional one who tries to wear scrubs. Have to inform them this isn't a surgical rotation. Only time I let them get by with it is if they've been on call the night before."

"Not me. I have better things to do with my energy than hassle medical students for wearing scrubs to clinic," said Trish "and why are we wasting our breath on such chit chat anyway?"

"Hey, you two! Keep it a little lower. Those blueheads at the next table are looking our way with disdainful glares," said Helen.

In a louder voice, Trish said, "By the way, Clare, how did your students like your lecture on sexual perversions? Did you show them those videos?"

"You joke!"

"I know," whispered Trish. "Wanted to see if there was a reaction."

"There is," whispered back Helen." Look, they're leaving. All six of the blue hairs are making a hasty exit."

"Oh, this place needs a little excitement every now and then. Boy, is the food good though! This champagne chicken breast is super," quipped Trish.

"What's in the stuffing?"

"Shrimp and artichoke, I think."

As the gals sipped their after-lunch, decaf coffee, Trish said, "We have some things to do next week. I can't get that strange tattoo out of my mind. Helen, you'll check out Voodoo Tattoo for us, and I will pump Sheila regarding gossip around the Medical School. And Barb, can you see what is floating around and pick up anything from the Ph.D. community. Clare, see what you can get on the autopsy? Talk to your buddy in Pathology, and I'll talk to our policeman, Clyde. When shall we meet again, girls?"

Clare replied, "In thunder, lightning or rain?"

"Don't be so dramatic," added Trish. "I know. Finding two corpses is a little creepy even to me, though I didn't exactly find the man on the beach."

"Say, I have an idea."

"What's that?"

"I have a conference call service on my phone. We could all talk without actually having to meet."

"Sounds great, and we can include Barb on the call. How about Wednesday night?" said Clare

"Okay, just wait until I get the kids in bed, say eight-thirty?" said Trish

"Great. Talk to you all then, but if something earth shaking comes up, don't make us wait," added Helen.

THIRTEEN

After a relatively hassle-free morning the next day, Trish finally found an opportunity to quiz Sheila without potential eavesdroppers about. "Sheila, what have heard about the Biochem fellow?"

"Not much, Dr. Trish. She was indeed a postdoc fellow. Dr. Weaver was her faculty supervisor even though he was also of pharmacology. She was Chinese and lived with several other foreign students in a duplex, over by Slattery Park and her name was Mi Ling."

"Such a pretty name. That's not a very good neighborhood."

"I know, but those kids have very limited resources and limited opportunity to earn any. Her housemates are distraught. She was cheerful, sweet, and well liked — an extremely hard worker. Sandra in Biochem said she and some of the others would be here until eleven or twelve many a night, and on weekends, too."

"I've always ascribed to *All work and no play make Jack a dull boy* myself."

"Me, too, but not these Chinese students."

"Were they all… how many did you say?"

"Four in the duplex."

"In Biochem?"

"No, only two. The others are in Physiology and one in Microbiology."

"I wonder if there is any way you could subtly find out if any of her housemates have a tattoo of a blue heart?"

"Why?"

"I noticed one on her body when I felt for a pulse. On her neck, behind her ear."

"I remember! That's intriguing. You told that to me and how it was the same design as on the research volunteer. I'll see what I can do and nose around some more."

"By the way, do you have any nail clippers? I have a hang nail."

Pulling open her desk drawer, Sheila pawed through a jumble of scissors, nail files, notepads, pens, and pencils for a minute and retrieved the nail clippers.

"Thanks. I'd be afraid to put my hand in there. Afraid of what might attack me."

"You know me, Dr. Trish, everything spiffy on the surface and somewhat of a clutter out of sight. I have great plans to someday have everything neat in all these drawers, but there's a part of me that is kind of afraid of that; if I have everything in order, I'll die."

"That's silly, Sheila! I hope you don't truly believe that."

"Oh, I don't, Dr. Trish. It's a thought that crosses my mind every now and then. My mind is pretty cluttered, too. Sometimes I wonder if I don't have a case of that attention deficit disorder I hear about."

"I doubt that, Sheila. But, if you are concerned, I could get someone at the clinic to check it out for you."

"Oh, it's not that bad. Probably being more like a sophomore medical student, thinking I have every disease I hear you doctors talk about, and lots of times I listen in on the Grand Rounds from the projection booth in the rear of the lecture hall and that gives me ideas."

"I don't think you need to worry. By the way, are your boys going to Scout Camp this summer?"

"Yep, but not until later in the summer. We'll be taking them up to North Carolina."

Trish picked up her mail and headed to her office; whereupon switching on the green glass shaded banker's lamp, she proceeded to scan, toss, or keep a pile of correspondence. There was a four-to-one ratio; four to toss and one to keep.

"Too bad we don't recycle paper around this joint," she mused and continued the task.

What is it with you and finding murder victims? It's hardly been a couple of years and now another one? Maybe we should have gone into Pathology.

No, never.

Anyway, you're not smart enough.

Well, I think we are if we wanted to.

You've never liked dead bodies. Remember what a relief it was to finish gross anatomy and pathology? Nowadays, I bet they don't even let medical students assist in autopsies.

Look, I was just being helpful when I found Hilda's body.

And now you were just being helpful when you discovered Mi Ling.

Maybe we're just curious; not so much helpful. Remember, Mary Lou had screamed there was a body, and I was curious as to what made her scream so. And, I was curious about the body on the beach and curious as to what the weather was doing when I went to the stairwell. Look, can we help it if dead bodies come across our paths? We don't know the cause of death of the young woman in the stairwell.

We're trying to just do normal things and then this. Of course, one option is to just leave these two alone.

What do you mean by that?

I must admit with our Lunch Bunch gang of four—Clare, Helen and Barb— I was running the show. Clare, you check on autopsy data, and Helen call the tattoo parlor, etc.

Okay, Okay. I'll admit I have a morbid curiosity about them, how and why they died.

So, what's wrong with that?

Nothing, I guess. As long as we just think about it and don't start doing anything stupid.

What do you mean by that?

Look. There are two dead people out there. This isn't New

Orleans. We don't have that many unexplained deaths around here, and they could be murder for all we know.

So?

I think they were both murdered.

Then someone who did the deeds is probably in the area.

No one but you has even considered that possibility.

You think there's a relationship?

Maybe yes, maybe no. But, both had a blue heart tattoo.

These deaths aren't the usual armed robbery gone bad or jealous husband/wife killings, or drug deal gone bad types.

There is something different here.

We don't even know the cause of death of the postdoc fellow as you said.

The man died of drowning. There's more than one way to drown; and why the bullet to the head if he was dead? He could have been held under.

We don't know the tox studies results, either.

What I'm saying is we now have a husband and two precious children to think about before we go off on some wild goose chase that might put them at risk.

Me? We're both in this together!

Okay, we know as a shrink, once a killing is committed, and especially if it's not from a state of passion, it would be much easier, or rather there would be less reluctance to kill again to achieve a goal.

What goal?

We don't know, do we?

But, people don't just go around killing people like swatting mosquitoes. That would have to be a real psycho, and there's not much chance of that.

But, why would two people with blue heart tattoos have unusual or unexplained deaths? Hell! I don't know! Why don't you talk to the other person you know with a blue heart tattoo.

Who's that?

The gal you saw in the Psychopharm Research Unit.

Oh, yeah! Maybe, I'll just do that.

Okay, let's cut this out. You need to do something to earn our pay.

❈

FOURTEEN

Trish scurried back to her office like a hound dog on a hot scent, closed the door, and immediately picked up her phone and called the Psychopharmacology Research Unit before she sat down and tilted back in her chair.

"Hi, this is Dr. Trish. Could you have a student worker bring me the file on Linda Lingo? She's a subject I saw last week. I need to review something in her file."

Should we be doing this?

No, but we're going to anyway.

One of these days your curiosity is going to get us in trouble.

It was just a brief five minutes later when the summer high school student worker gave a timid knock on the door and delivered the file.

"Thanks, Stacey, for being so prompt. Please wait. This won't take a minute." Trish quickly jotted the name, address, and phone number from the file and returned it to the waiting girl, who was doing a survey of the office and the certificates and plaques that lined one wall.

"Here you go. That's all I need. Thanks."

"No problem Dr. Trish. It's neat to see the office of a real professor."

So, what are you going to do with her name, address, and phone number? Call her?

Of course not. She wasn't accepted for the study anyway.

When the lab results came back, her fasting blood sugar was borderline elevated. But, I think either Barb or Helen can do a little checking for our group. Probably Helen, since she's not med-ical. I'll call her tonight.

Clare knocked and stuck her head in the door as Trish was gathering her purse and tote bag.

"How's tricks?"

"No complaints, Clare. I'm about off to the Middling…I mean Mental Health Clinic. I have students this afternoon."

"Trish, is it just me or does there seem to be a lot more traffic down our hall today?"

"It's not just you, Clare. I think there are a number of jerks who want to see where the body was found."

"At least some of them pretend to be on a walkabout with athletic shoes, but it's really thinly-veiled curiosity."

"I'm going to ask Helen to see what she can find out about the volunteer we had for a clinical research project, the one who had a blue heart tattoo. We did all the preliminary work and then she was scratched when the labs showed an elevated fasting glucose level. I'm off!"

"Talk to you later."

No students were in sight when Trish entered her part-time office at the community Mental Health Clinic that she shared with other faculty.

At least something is running smoothly. This group had enough sense to go ahead and start seeing the patients.

A short twenty minutes later the first two students came in and presented their patient.

"Ms. Hurst is a fifty-year-old white female with a twenty-year history of depression. Last hospitalization, the result of an overdose, occurred over ten years ago…"

The students plowed ahead with agonizing detail, includ-ing the patient's current mental status, concluding with the recommendation she continue taking her current level of antidepressants.

"Okay, good job. Let's go see her."

The students led the way, and Trish briefly interviewed the patient and signed the prescriptions already filled out by the students, as well as their progress note, and wrote a short note herself indicating that she agreed with the students, along with a few comments and observations of her own. Upon her return to the office, another pair of students was waiting to present. The afternoon went smoothly for once. In total, the four pairs of students saw eight patients. All were stable, and none was having any undue side effects from medication.

"What a blessed afternoon this has been," thought Trish as she pulled out of the parking lot about 4:45.

Can't remember when we've had an afternoon go this well

It won't last.

These were all outstanding students, and, come to think of it, none of the patients had borderline personality disorders or traits. Those are the ones who make for drama, complaints, and acting out. Next week we'll probably have five out of eight and have to admit one. It seems there is a waxing and waning of difficulties. If I could just deduce the rhythm and predict it, we could make a fortune.

As she pulled into the garage, Trish noted Steven's blue Expedition in place radiating significant heat.

He's not long here.

"Hi, anybody here?" she called.

Little Adam came running out the door to his mama's arms.

"Mommy, Mommy, I potty like a big boy today. Throw away the diapers."

"Wow! That's wonderful. Is this true?" she said to Steven who was leaning against the entry to the den, Amy in his arms.

Grinning, he said, "For real. He's doing it. Mercedes said it was all of a sudden."

"Thank God for small favors. I was having visions of sending pull-ups with him to first grade."

"Trish, now that he's potty trained, he can go to Mother's

Day out at church a couple of mornings a week. He'll think it's school, and he'll have other kids to play with."

"Good idea, Steven. Is supper ready?"

"Yep. Mercedes said all was ready. We only need to make a salad and put ice in glasses for tea, so I told her she could go home."

"Okay, let me change clothes and wash my hands. How's my baby girl?" Giving Amy a quick snuggle and a kiss, she returned her to Steven.

"She'll be satisfied in her swing if you want to start on the salad."

"No problem. Come help Daddy, Adam." Adam followed Steven into the kitchen where he assisted by tearing the stems from several spinach leaves. Steven lined up items for the salad and let Adam pick what to use.

"Dat and dat and dat and dat and dat," said Adam.

Before he stopped, Steven said, "Why am I letting you choose? You don't eat salad anyway. You've pointed to olives — you hate them — picked cauliflower, artichoke, and dill pickles. That's too much. We'll use cherry tomatoes, artichoke hearts, and croutons."

Adam agreeably chirped, "Okey dokey," and ran to the table and climbed into his booster chair, taking his personal child-sized fork and spoon in hand and said, "Eat now!"

"Right away, Champ," said Trish, now fresh in twill khaki shorts and aqua gingham check blouse, placed Amy in the highchair adjacent to her place.

"Want to say a blessing, Champ?" Steven asked.

Adam piped back, "Jesus love me."

"That will do, I guess. He learned that in Sunday School."

"How was your day, Trish?"

"Actually, great. No major fires to extinguish and this block of junior students are very good, probably because they'll be seniors in a couple of weeks and have learned some things along the way. And you?"

"Sam approached me regarding the Cross Gulf Race. Wanted to know if I was interested in crewing."

"What did you say?"

"Not my cup of tea anymore. I'm satisfied with day sailing, maybe a little local race every now and then. So things have calmed down at the Medical School? You're not going to resign?"

"I haven't decided yet. Today was a little more even; however, it's simply a lull, and I know it. There's a real concern around the Medical Center as to how someone could die, and I think be killed, right in the Medical School building."

"Don't they have security video cameras all over the place?"

"Yes, they do. But this area where the poor girl, Mi Ling, was found is a 'dead area' of the building, with little traffic, and in an area where there is no video surveillance. They will, I am sure, check the videos of the night or even the day before; but if her death was planned, what I mean is, if the videos are not very sophisticated, and it wouldn't take much to make one useless."

"Are you concerned about your personal safety? I am a little worried for you."

"I do not stay after five or five-thirty at the latest and never go in the Medical School on weekends. When I have weekend rounds with the residents, I enter and leave via the hospital and don't use the parking garage. I do find it creepy without people about. It would have to be a very unusual circumstance for me to be in that garage or that part of the school after regular hours."

"Okay, but it pays to be aware of your surroundings wherever you are. Remember Nancy from church; kidnapped right in the Wal-Mart parking lot at 11:00 a.m. a couple of years ago?"

"No problem, I can do that. I do it now. Helen is going to stop by the Voodoo Tattoo parlor and see what she can learn about a blue heart tattoo."

"Whoa, Voodoo Tattoo Parlor? Hope you gals aren't getting into something you shouldn't."

"Oh, we're just checking on a few things; nothing serious."

"Let's hope so. Better leave murder investigations to the authorities, the experts."

"That may not always be effective. If we gals hadn't intervened, Hilda Rasberry's killer would have gotten away Scotfree. Remember how we were involved in that even if we were behind the scene?"

"You know the old saying *Curiosity killed the cat* and sometimes you can be very catlike."

"Meow, purr, purr, purr," said Trish as she smiled at Steven.

❋

FIFTEEN

"Hi, it's me."

"Oh, hi, Trish."

"What's up, Helen?"

"Reggie is asleep in his recliner. As I told you the other day, I'm afraid he's drinking again. I hope you agree I did the right thing. I called his sponsor. I'm not supposed to know who it is, but he let it slip. He was real nice-sounding man and said he would talk to him. By the way, to change the subject, the catering business is going great. However, what is going on with you?"

"An okay day at school and the clinic for me. Say did you have time to phone or stop by the Voodoo Tattoo Studio?"

"I didn't stop by, but I called and chatted with a nice gal. She sounded oriental on the phone. I acted like I was interested in getting a tattoo. I didn't tell her my name. She said they will do almost anything a person wants, and in any color, although some colors tend to fade more."

"Did you ask about blue hearts?"

"Yes, in a roundabout way. It appears hearts are very popular, but most always are red. She didn't know of any blue ones done at her shop. But, an interesting thing is, I was chatting in the checkout line at Winn-Dixie, and this cute young woman with a baby ahead of me, had a blue heart tattoo."

"No kidding? Of course, you asked about her tattoo and where she got it?"

"How'd you guess?"

"Just lucky, I guess."

"But that wasn't what I wanted to tell you. She knew of the Voodoo Tattoo studio and said the owner was an ex-policeman from Mobile."

"That is strange. Why would someone stop being a policeman to open a tattoo studio? I know policemen don't make a lot of money, but I'm not so sure how much a tattoo shop would make either. I don't think it's of any importance to us, but you never know. Maybe this tattoo place is a front for other business that is ten times more lucrative than that of a simple shopkeeper or policeman?"

"What kind of front?"

"Beats me. Maybe drugs?"

"Whatever. Maybe he is providing papers for illegal aliens. I do think someone needs to actually go by the place and look and see what kind of equipment they have, how the people look, get a feel for the place, maybe take a picture of a blue heart tattoo and ask how much it would cost to do one like that."

"So far we know of three women with the tattoo. Mi Ling, who is dead, the reject volunteer from the Psycho Pharm Study, and the gal you saw in the line at the grocery."

"Then, the body the authorities found on the Gulf beach had one."

"That's right. I need to call Clyde. Bye now."

SIXTEEN

"Clyde? Trish here."

"Oh, I recognize you by now, Dr. Trish. What's up?"

"Sorry to call you at home."

"No problem."

"Say, did the police get an ID on that poor man washed up on the beach?"

"They're running fingerprints on him, but nothing back as yet. He may be an alien after all."

"What about his clothes? Were they foreign made?"

"Don't know, Dr. Trish, but most, or a lot, of clothing sold in our stores is produced overseas, so that might not be of much help. He didn't have any jewelry, but I'm sort of embarrassed to tell you, the fellow had only one testicle."

"Do you make anything of that?"

"The post said there was a scar, so it had been removed surgically. There wasn't one inside him, either. It's fairly well known drug or jewel smugglers hide their products in there."

"Clyde, as far as I know, one testicle is not removed unless there is something wrong with it, disease or some strange trauma, but that smuggling idea is something I've never considered. Most interesting."

"Unless something comes back on his prints, this will be written off as Closed."

"Anything from Missing Persons?"

"Nope."

"I guess it is over — still, that strange blue heart tattoo. Stay in touch."

"Sure thing."

SEVENTEEN

The Voodoo Tattoo studio was a throwback to the hippy life style of the 60's. Examples of tattoo designs covered the walls, as well as photos of clients exhibiting the artwork on various parts of their bodies.

"Hello there. Can I help you?" It was a red-haired woman who looked as though she had stuck her finger into an electric outlet as she turned from a blaring television.

She looks like a witch.

Maybe not, could be eccentric or a member of a cult.

"Oh, I was curious about your tattoo parlor," said Trish.

"You're welcome to look around. Only nowadays we are called a tattoo studio. The term parlor went out in the 1960's. Many of our tattooists are artists in their own right, as you can see by examples of their work."

"Yes, some of these are works of art. You or your people design these?"

"Yes, some, but not all. Now, Sid, he's a real artist. Works in other mediums also. He can make up a design unique for you."

"Oh, I'm not personally in the market."

Maybe it would be fun. Ol' Steven might like it. Might really turn him on.

Hush! He's turned on enough already.

"What kind of folks come here for a tattoo?"

"All kinds — young and old, from every stratum of life. You might be surprised, but 75% of our customers are women."

"For true? Do they get these elaborate designs?"

"Some do, but many get a small design like a rose or heart or their zodiac sign."

"Heart?"

"Yes, they are popular. We do a lot of small ones on the breast."

"How interesting. What color?"

"Red, almost always."

"Ever have anyone request a blue heart, a dark sapphire blue in a design not quite shaped like a Valentine?"

"I can't say for sure 'cause I only work part-time, but Sid the owner might have. Why do you ask?"

"No reason in particular. A friend saw a gal in line at the checkout line at Winn-Dixie with a small blue heart on the side of her neck and thought she might want one. But my friend is the kind of person who wouldn't want one if it were popular. She always goes for the unique and unusual."

Just then, a tall, slender to the point of being skinny, man in cutoffs and a tie-dyed t-shirt came into the room from a rear office.

"Hello. How are you doing, Ma'am?"

"Oh, hi. Fine, thank you. *This must be Sid. Look at those tattoos all over his arms and legs.* This place looks like a real art gallery. I was just asking some questions about your work."

"Sure. What can I tell you?"

"Oh, how long have you been doing this?"

"You mean tattoos or owner of a tattoo studio?"

"Both."

"Been doing tattoos 'bout twenty years or so. Used to be a policeman, but my heart wasn't in it. Opened this shop about three years ago, and I can tell you, last year I made five times what I made as a policeman. That was the gross. Of course, I have my overhead, and I pay several artists to work for me, and Ramona, here, helps out part-time."

As Ramona smiled, she jingled from stacks of bracelets and long dangling earrings. She had a metal belt with long tendrils that jangled, over a long broomstick skirt. The combination looked strange to Trish, with the woman's white athletic shoes without socks, new and clean. The cotton peasant blouse, low-cut, revealed a two-inch rose tattoo in red, with a couple of green leaves poking from behind the blossom.

"Actually, I'm Sid's sister-in-law," she said, "but I like the studio, and we have such an interesting clientele. I am even somewhat of an artist myself. Not near what Sid here is, but I can do a nice job if it's not too complicated, huh, Sid?"

"Yep. She's right, and some of the ladies prefer a woman to do their tattoo."

"Let me show you what my friend saw on the woman. May I?"

"Sure."

Trish then sketched the off-center heart Helen had described and she herself had observed on Mi Ling's body.

"Ever do anything like this?"

Sid took a look at the design. "It certainly is a slightly different shape for a heart than I've done, and you said she wanted it to be blue?"

"Not necessarily so. The one she saw on the gal at Winn-Dixie happened to be blue."

"I don't recall doing this design, but I do have a number of books you can look through," and he pulled a rather ancient dog-eared volume from the shelf behind the counter. "Here, let's look and see what we can find."

He flipped through the pages. "Yep, here's a bunch of hearts. Want to look? Most of these are fairly simple; only cost you twenty or thirty bucks."

He thinks I want one and is softening me up for a sale.

Trish turned the pages. There were several designs on each page, but none resembled the design on Mi Ling's neck. Then, on the last page, below a title, 'Mystic Designs from the East,' was the heart. And lo and behold, it was blue. A handwritten note indicated, 'This design is to be only in a dark, sapphire blue.'

"That's it!" exclaimed Trish. "Is this your book? Do you know anything about this one?"

Sid perused the page and replied, "It's my book. I picked it up in a garage sale a few years back for twenty-five cents, so I don't know where it came from. I don't remember ever using this design. What about you, Ramona? Ever do this one?" and he showed her the page.

"No, but it is kind of nice. I might like to do it, as it's different and more artistic than the ones I do. Would you like me to do it for you?"

No way! Stay polite.

" Not now, I'll think about it and get back to you."

"We use sterile techniques here. I insist on it. Don't want to be passing any diseases around. You'll not find a cleaner place; not even a hospital," Sid said proudly.

"I'm sure you're telling the truth, but today I only wanted some information and I'll think about it. If any of your artists are familiar with the blue heart design, please let me know," and Trish jotted her home phone number on a slip of paper.

"It's really my friend who's interested in a tattoo, not me. I'll be running along now."

"Honey, I'll be glad to do it for you anytime," Ramona said as Trish departed the studio.

Well, what do we think about that little encounter?

What do you mean by that? Looks like a dead-end to me.

Maybe not. We did learn they call the tattoo places 'studios' not 'parlors,' and that a lot of them are actually artists.

That's not much help in the mystery. At least we did see the design in that old book.

Now, I'm curious as to what are 'Mystic Designs from the East?'

That could be anything.

Someone could make up the name to give the impression the designs were exotic.

Or maybe some people would think the sign denoted magical power or protection.

We're really reaching now, aren't we?

Look, we know our best thinking when one of us is curious happens when we think, act, or feel outside the box. This is, for sure, a time for that.

Why are we always so curious?

Beats me. It's the way God made us. Been that way since we were very little. We know being curious made us a good psychotherapist.

We have to be thankful, true. Another thought just came to mind. Maybe it's a symbol of some group or clan or something like that? Or even a family?

We could do some research on the Web about 'Mystical Signs from the East' and see.

Okay, I'll ask Barb Bonno to do that for our group. She's always doing searches for her forensic toxicology legal cases.

That's a great idea from you for once!

And, after all, she's a member of our Lunch Bunch sleuth team.

She helped on the solving of the murder of Hilda Rasberry.

❁

EIGHTEEN

"Hi, Barb, it's me."

"Sure, Trish, what's up?"

"Have you heard anything on the rumor mill at school about Mi Ling's death?"

"Not much. I ran into Joye Lynn — she dates one of the guys who work in the morgue — while I was in the restroom to freshen up, so as usual, I pumped her. Somehow I figured you'd be calling me to see if I had heard anything.'"

"What made you think that?"

"Now, Trish. How long have we been friends?"

"Quite a few years. I forget how many."

"And, I've never known anyone who is innately as curious about whatever comes down the pike as you. I bet when you were a little girl, you drove your mama and aunts crazy with 'Why? Why? Why?'"

"Come to think of it, at the last visit with mama and Aunt Hazel, they were talking about that very thing. But, in my defense, it has been useful as a researcher and psychotherapist to be curious. So, what did Felicia tell you? By the way, she has the most gorgeous green eyes. Guess it's her biracial heredity."

"Here's the scoop. Felicia said Justin her boyfriend overheard a couple of the Path faculty chatting about that funny tattoo."

"The heart you mean?"

"I think so, but they weren't calling it a heart."

"That's what it looked like to me, just skewed, like they drew it in a hurry."

"He overheard them say it was a professional job; not any do-it-yourself one or like prisoners do on themselves, and that one of the pathologists said it appeared to be two separate lines. That at first glance it appeared to be joined top and bottom. But if one looked at it from a different angle, like the near point at the top, it took on an entirely different form, not a heart, but maybe two horns, like antlers or exotic animal horns."

"That's a new angle. What do you make of that?"

"Nothing much."

"Listen, you do a lot of searches. Do you think you could come up with something off the Web? Symbols and all that? Hell, it might be some kind of letter or even a word in some unknown language."

"That's really thinking outside the box, but it's worth a run. I'll have to do it at home unless I can think of a legit way to do it at school. I need to set a good example."

"Good example?"

"Sure. We aren't supposed to do personal searches on university computers."

"Yeah, I remember, not that I've ever had time to do much other than check the weather."

"You'd be surprised. There are people around the building who spend hours playing games and searching e-Bay for whatever. They'd better be careful, especially with porno sites. Who knows what internal audit will decide to look at? Remember that guy in Micro who got fired last year?"

"Who?"

"Dr. Sapho."

"Yeah. They thought he was up to some funny business and took his computer down to Computer Services for a good look-see. I never knew what that was all about, but it wasn't long after that he was 'Gone with the Wind.' Say, I just had another idea. Do you know anyone on the faculty over at the college, say someone in the History Department?"

"I'll ask around. Clare or Helen may."

"Okay, I'll ask them. If we can show the design to a history buff, we might get a new idea."

"How's the family?"

"Terrific. Steven isn't too happy over my interest in this girl's death, which I think may be a murder. By the way, have you heard of the cause of death?"

"Not yet. Bet they've sent specimens off for exotic lab tests. I'll keep my ear to the ground on it, though. So, you check with Clare and Helen regarding a history buff, and I'll run a search on symbols to start with. Catch you later."

That was interesting about looking at things from a different angle.

What do you mean?

Turning that heart around the other way. It could be two antlers, or even some strange letter. Curious, isn't it?

That's for sure.

NINETEEN

"Helen, honey? Trish here."

"Oh, hi, Trish. How's tricks?" Helen continued painting her toenails a bright rose pink as she hooked the phone under her ear.

"Great! Listen, would you happen to know any faculty members over at the college who are history buffs?"

"I might. I'll ask Reggie, too. What's up?"

"The heart tattoo on both corpses might not be a heart after all."

"Not a heart?"

"Yes, if you look at the design from another angle, it might be antlers or a strange letter or some other symbol."

"You're so clever! How did you come up with that?"

"It wasn't me. The idea came from someone else. Could you check for us on a history buff?"

"Sure thing. I'm taking a World History course this fall. Thought I would finally get a degree, so I'll be going over there anyway."

"Great. Keep me posted."

"Sure thing. Love ya. Bye now."

"Bye, love ya, Helen."

❀

TWENTY

The massive mausoleum of the Medical School — at least it held death the day Mi Ling was murdered, if Trish was correct in her suspicion — awakened in the early morning a sleeping giant adjacent to the University Hospital that in contrast, hummed with life throughout the night. The sounds were familiar to Trish as she noted the click of her high heels on the terrazzo floor, echoing off the closed office and lab doors. As she passed, a few labs with open doors shed streams of fluorescent coolness into the hall.

"Gee, must be a little early this morning. The hall lights are still on dim," she said out loud to herself. Just then, as she arrived at her office door, the hall lights came on with a brilliant glare, reflecting a bluish sheen off the polished floor. Adjusting the floral silk wreath on her door, Trish inserted her key and turned it. *Funny, it isn't working. Hell, the door's open! Those housekeeping staff sometimes are so slack. Remember, they don't get paid much, and some are far from the sharpest knife in the drawer.*

Trish snapped on the office fluorescent light and the green glass banker's lamp on her desk. *You could be a little neater. Shut up! It's not too bad this morning. Look, the desk is neat.*

What about the rest?

What's this?

Housekeeping must have dusted.

I don't think so. The empty space on the desk is dusty, and there's a ring where I spilled my spiced tea last week. Things are definitely rearranged. I had my crystal snail over here by the phone. You know I like to touch it when I'm talking on the phone. Oh, my! What? The desk is unlocked! No way? Yep, and I'm certain I locked it when I left. Who else has a key? Only Martha.

A small folded note of card stock quality paper lay in the bottom of the right hand drawer where Trish usually stowed her bulky Coach purse.

What's this?

Trish unfolded the note to read in crisp block letters, the words MIND YOUR OWN BUSINESS.

A chill ran up her spine and she glanced at the door and picked up the phone. *Damn! None of the support staff is here yet. They don't come until 8:30, remember? Sure, sure, but this weird.*

Trish picked up the note and placed it on top of the desk. *I've read that sometimes specialists can get fingerprints off even something like this. I'm sure it's expensive, so why would they do it? No crime has been committed unless they broke into your office and desk. You probably left it unlocked. You have before, and the cleaners go around and open a whole series of offices at a time. Remember, Barb told you that. She was shocked to discover it when she came back on a Saturday to pick up something.*

I don't care; this is creepy.

It was a few minutes later when Trish heard Sheila's footsteps down the hall pause and the door to her office close. *It's interesting how I can tell who's coming by the sound of their footsteps, except if they're wearing soft soles.*

Picking up the note, Trish exited her office and headed to Sheila's.

"How's my favorite secretary this morning?"

"Since I'm the only one you have, great. What's up?" replied Sheila as Trish handed her the note.

"What do you make of this?"

"Depends on who it's from and who it's to."

"Me, Sheila. I found it in the bottom of the drawer where I keep my purse. And the desk and door to my office were unlocked when I arrived this morning."

"Housekeeping must have left the door unlocked, but you're pretty good about locking your desk."

"Sure am. I even lock it when I just go down to the coffee shop or bookstore. Sheila, this gives me the creeps."

"What have you done to get a note like this?"

"Nothing that I can tell. Oh, Clare, Helen, Barb and I have had a few chats about Mi Ling's death. I think she may have been killed. She was apparently a healthy young woman. These were only discussions. We're as curious as everyone else, and I did check out a tattoo studio for a little background. I was wondering about the heart tattoo."

"Don't go getting paranoid over a little note. It may just be a joke."

"Some joke. Is Martha the only other one who has a key to my desk?"

"Yep, as far as I know. But I'm sure someone who knows how and had the proper equipment would have no problem opening the desk."

"I'll be out over lunch today. I'm meeting Steven. We seldom have a meal just the two of us without the kids. So I'll discuss this with him."

"Are you leaving the Medical Center for lunch?"

"No, he's coming here. We'll just be in the Atrium eating super salads from the Deli."

❃

TWENTY-ONE

"Hungry?" said Steven as he walked up behind Trish and kissed her neck.

Trish jumped, startled, "Don't scare me like that! Sure. I'm starved."

"Scare you? What's up?"

Trish turned, giving him a hug, saying, "I'll tell you about it at lunch. Just let me lock my desk, and we can go down to the Salad Bar."

The doctors' dining area was filling fast; however, Steven spied a remaining corner table and was quick to say, "You okay, honey? I've never seen you jump like that. Let's eat here."

"You're right. I am a little on edge. Look at this." And she pulled the note from her pocket.

As he read it, Steven said, "Where'd this come from?"

Trish explained.

"Are you sure you gals aren't getting into deep water talking about that poor girl's death and thinking it murder?"

"I don't see how, but I was sure my desk and office were locked, and we're not doing anything much; just a little research on tattoo symbols."

"Tattoo symbols?"

"Remember? I told you she had a blue heart tattoo on her neck and Helen saw a gal in Winn-Dixie with one; and then I saw a volunteer for a research project with one, and there was another research volunteer rejected for a study who had one."

"So?"

"So, we're curious about seeing blue heart tattoos and to

boot, they are the shape of the sapphire you bought me in Hong Kong."

"Let it rest, Trish."

So the lunch continued with no further speculations. "This salad isn't half bad," said Trish "Not much of a way to screw it up when you assemble it yourself."

"I'll see you tonight. Relax, Trish. Chill out. It is probably nothing to be concerned about."

Trish wasn't too sure about that and found her self frowning as she made her way back to her office so preoccupied she did not speak to any one she passed in the halls.

Back in the department, Trish found Sheila in a tizzy. Several medical students just finishing the block were asking about their evaluations; the student worker was shuffling papers in between several phone calls and taking messages. She was struggling to cope.

"Let the voicemail take the calls and I'll take care of them," said Sheila as Sophia, a third year resident, was asking about her prior approval for a meeting three months away.

Trish stood observing the maelstrom as she perused her box for messages. Sheila was amazing, a juggler in action. "You should join the circus, Sheila."

"What?"

"The way you juggle five or six things at a time. I'll check with you later when things calm down."

"Oh, I wish, Dr. Trish. This is just a notch above the norm and this time, a bunch of the student evals were signed by residents. That won't fly, and some idiot marked just a letter grade with no comments. They'll all have to be redone in the correct form and with a faculty member signing them. You would think they could read the instructions, and to think these guys are training doctors to take care of my health in my old age!"

"Calm down, Sheila." Trish stopped as a slip of paper fell from the stack of mail in her arms. Picking it up, she read once again MIND YOUR OWN BUSINESS. Shocked, she swallowed, frowned, and hurried to her office.

Now, where was that other one? Did you throw it away? No, I think I just put it in the drawer. Yep, here it is. They're the same. How strange? I can't imagine what these are about.

"Somebody doesn't like me for sure," she whispered under her breath. Comparing the two, she realized they weren't copies. The letters were slightly different. Worried, Trish questioned herself because she prided herself on not meddling in the affairs of others and was surprised to note she was feeling hurt and a little sad. She remembered feeling the same way as a child. Or was it as a teenager when she had suggested, in all innocence, to an aunt whom she adored, how she should arrange furniture in her bedroom? Trish seldom saw this aunt as she lived several hundred miles away, but adored her and thought the feelings were reciprocated. The aunt had broken her toe when she tripped on a dresser leg going to the bathroom during the night.

I only was suggesting that if she changed the arrangement, she wouldn't run the risk of breaking something again. I felt surprised and hurt; yes, hurt. Trish felt tears come to her eyes. *That's just the way I feel now.*

That's stupid; why feel sad? Why not be mad? Why feel either?

I really thought I was over that reaction. I learned in my therapy years ago to ask the other person if they wanted a suggestion before giving advice. And darn, I have done a good job at that in my life. Wow! Now I'm angry. But, here, there is no one to ask, and what to ask about anyway. What have I said or done that someone thinks isn't my business? How can I correct and leave something alone when I have no idea what it is? Maybe Steven will have some ideas.

You know, you're avoiding something. What are you shoving back in our mind? Let it bubble up.

Okay, it's this new curiosity about Mi Ling's death.

There's someone who resents your curiosity about her death.

Could Clare or Barb have mentioned to someone around the Medical Center that we have been discussing her death?

Trish picked up the phone and entered Clare's pager number through her exchange. She closed her eyes as she waited for the return ring. It was only a couple of minutes.

"Clare?"

"Yes?"

"Listen, something has happened. Could you stop by my office this afternoon after you finish C-L rounds? Do you have very many to see today? Great? No, it's not that pressing. See ya, say, four or so? Okay. Bye."

She turned to her computer and proceeded to work on a PowerPoint presentation for a resident lecture scheduled the following month. Trish definitely was not a person to wait until the last minute on assignments.

It was four straight up when Clare knocked.

"Enter, Clare. I recognize your knock," said Trish as Clare stuck her long, bobbed, ash-blonde head around the door frame.

"What's up? It's rare for you to page me?"

Trish showed the two cards to Clare. "What do you make of these?"

"Not much. Where did they come from?"

"One was in my mailbox and one on my desk."

"Have you gone in someone's office or lab uninvited?"

"No, of course not."

"I wouldn't worry, Trish. Probably just a practical joke; you of all people — other people's business?"

"I agree, except as a therapist."

"Then that is your business as the patient's psychiatrist."

"I have been curious about the death of poor Mi Ling. But, hell, I haven't done any real investigating. I happened to discover the body. By the way, heard any more about her?"

"Yes, I have. She was, as we know, a postdoc, but guess who she was working with?"

"Who?"

"Weaver."

"Wesley Weaver, the other leprechaun?"

"Dr. Parker's twin. None other. Trish, I've never liked that twerp. How he got a dual faculty appointment, I'll never know."

"Of course you do; it's his degree from Cambridge. He makes me sick with that British accent of his. Rumor is, he is really bucking for an endowed chair. Can't just be satisfied with his research perks. Bet he was a pill to work under. Wonder what they were working on?"

"I'm not sure, but I overheard some physiology students at the next table in the cafeteria say she was on to something really brilliant. Big-time stuff that would put ol' Weaver in the shade."

"That certainly wouldn't sit well with the leprechaun. He has a little-man complex, if you ask me. He's probably a lush, too. I observed that a couple of years ago at a faculty wives affair. He was rude and kept putting down his wife in public. Called her a stupid bitch."

"No way! We don't hear talk like that 'round here much, if ever. Trish, back to Mi Ling. Maybe she wasn't killed, only died there in the stairwell. Remember, there is access to that stairwell from the library below. Maybe she was feeling sick and went out there for some fresh air, or to talk to someone in private."

"About what?"

"Hell, I don't know."

"What are they saying about cause of death now?"

"Some kind of respiratory failure. Possibly arrhythmia leading to cardiac arrest, but nothing significant showed up on the slides."

"Anything unusual in gastric contents?"

"Nope. She had salad fragments. She didn't chew her food very well. Had red beans in there, too. Since she was found here, McInnis okayed the post to be performed by one of our faculty pathologists. They don't do nearly as many as in past years, and McInnis has his hands full with low funding and big demands."

"I'd better close up this shop for the day. Keep in touch, Clare."

"Sure thing. I've got to stop by Winn-Dixie on the way home anyway. You know, of course, there is a memorial service for Mi Ling tomorrow in the hospital chapel?"

"No, what time?"

"Noon. Want to sit together?"

"Okay. I really didn't know her."

"But you did find her body."

"Okay, we can observe who shows up. Listen, see if you can ask around about exactly what she was working on."

❁

TWENTY-TWO

It was after the kids were in bed before Trish had a chance to tell Steven her concerns about the notes.

"Do you think there's anything to it?" she asked.

"Probably not."

"I've never had anything like this happen to me. I'm just a regular person who happens to teach in the Medical School. My life is supposed to be calm and serene."

"That's a laugh. From what you tell me, Trish, that Medical Center is a cesspool of stress and power struggles. The way you guys fight over space offices, clinics, and parking slots reminds me of range wars between the cattlemen and the sheep herders."

"That's true. I noticed last week there's an office that five years ago was a storage closet."

"How could that be, Trish?"

"It was a large closet. They just put in a fluorescent light and keep the door open for ventilation."

"Wonder what kind of office the postdoc — Mi Ling — had?"

"Not much, I'm sure. Maybe a desk in a corner of Weaver's lab or a desk in a room with several other staff."

"Have they decided the cause of her death yet?"

"I talked to Clare and she said that so far it looks like cardiac arrest. But, she was young for that. Of course, the slides and tox studies aren't back yet. One interesting thing; she had quite a bit of saliva coming out of her mouth, and her clothes were damp, as if she were really sweating heavily just before death. But, people who have heart attacks do at times have saliva from the mouth. Unless there was something unusual about her death, why would anyone bother to write those notes to me?"

"Could be the notes have nothing to do with Mi Ling's death. Ever consider that, Trish?"

"Uh huh. So what else am I involved in around school that would cause the notes? Maybe some committee I'm on? There are enough of those."

"Maybe not a committee. Remember, you are a great one for putting together pieces that seem to have no relationship to each other, into something significant. There was that big flap a while back when you saw Dr. Weaver dining at that expensive restaurant we went to celebrate our anniversary? Only you would note the label on the wine bottles at his table and later check to find they were $100 each."

"Steven, it wasn't one bottle. There were four or five on the table. It looked cluttered. In a place like that, the waiter is supposed to remove each bottle as it is emptied. I was curious how the leprechaun could afford that. His salary isn't so different from mine. Then it turned out he was misusing some of his grant money. I heard he was really pissed off when he got caught with his hand in the cookie jar. Some grants are pretty lenient as to how the money is used. Can I help it if an audit showed it?"

"If Weaver knew you tipped off the auditors, he would really be angry and think it wasn't your business."

"Steven, I didn't purposefully go tell anyone. I must have just mentioned that I saw him at The Pier restaurant, and the word passed around and the auditors decided to check. Anyway, I'm glad he was caught. I heard he's being considered for an endowed chair. He doesn't deserve that. He always climbs on the shoulders of his graduate students' work, if you ask me."

"I suggest you let it go. The woman probably died of natural causes and just happened to work with someone you don't like."

"Okay, but I'll still think about it. Why was she in that stairwell?"

❈

TWENTY-THREE

The tiny hospital chapel was packed when Trish arrived and signed the book outside the door. Unable to find a seat, she stood in the back with Clare and Barb during the brief service.

"'Pears she was a Christian," whispered Barb. "Not many of our Asian students are."

Afterwards, as they walked back to the Medical School together, Clare said, "Who do you think that sad-looking young man was?"

"Heard he was engaged to her. He's a grad student in Cellular Immunology," replied Barb.

"There certainly were a lot of nice things said about her. From the eulogies given by her roommates, it would seem a brilliant, sweet life was cut short. It might be interesting to talk to her roommates and fiancé about her health and if anyone didn't like her."

"I thought you were going to not get involved again in an unexpected death? This is just a tragedy, and after those two notes, do you think you should?"

"I'm not getting involved, only curious, and I don't know if the notes have anything to do with her death. It won't hurt to talk to one or two of her roommates."

"Hey gang, look who has beat us to the elevators," whispered Trish. It was Wesley Weaver, Ph.D., standing with a group of techs and students.

Dr. Weaver (never Wes or Wesley) stood out in a crowd. Barely five feet three, he was rotund with a ruddy red face and nose that bore more than a few alcohol related spider veins. His rusty red hair and piercing blue eyes under heavy bushy brows brought a second glance from those who passed by. In his white lab coat — too long for his body — he looked like a stuffed duck; partly because he buttoned it up.

"At Cambridge…" was all Trish heard as she waited at the rear of the group. Under her breath, she whispered to Clare and Barb, "You'd think he was God's personal emissary come to the Gulf Coast to give us poor things bits of his wisdom. The way he goes on. If he's so great, why's he here and not in the Northeast?"

"Maybe he likes to be a big frog in a little pond."

"It's more like he belongs in a swamp," replied Trish.

"Or a cesspool, better yet," chimed in Barb.

As the elevator doors closed, Weaver's clipped British accent continued his diatribes on how Mi Ling would be missed.

"At least we didn't have to ride the same elevator with him," quipped Clare.

"What time do you want to round, Dr. Conner?" It was one of the medical students assigned to Psych Consultation, on the next elevator they all took.

"Didn't see you there, Dave," replied Clare, "Come by the office about three. How many do we have for today?"

"Only three new ones and three follow-ups from yesterday,"

"We should finish by five easily, unless you get any more."

"Okay, thanks, Dr. Clare," he said stepping off on the second floor.

❁

"Do you think he heard what we were saying?" asked Barb.

"Probably not," said Trish. "We were talking under our breaths, and most medical students think the same thing about 'Weasel Weaver.'"

"Weasel? That's choice," said Clare. "Is that his new name? Might as well be. It sure fits him."

Back in her office, Trish called Sheila, and asked her to get the name and phone number for the young man who had been identified as Mi Ling's fiancé. It was an hour later when Sheila called Trish to report.

"His name is Su Quan, and he's a grad student in Microbiology, not Cellular Immunology. I called Doll, my contact in Biochem. She said he was another of the group of quiet, shy, hard-working Asian students. He was friends with a couple of the techs in the Psych Department even; usually had coffee break together, although he drank tea with them."

"Oh, who is that?"

"You know one of them, David."

"Oh, him. His name really isn't David, is it? I can't pronounce his Chinese name, so he said to call him David; it would be his American name. I've even eaten lunch with him a couple of times when he came to a Case Conference. Nice fellow. Thanks, Sheila." *Think I'll get myself invited to a coffee break with him. Nothing ventured, nothing gained.*

I'm going to be subtle about this, thought Trish as she walked to the Clinical Psychopharm Unit of the department where she interviewed and examined two new volunteers for a clinical trial of a new anti-anxiety drug. The unit was only a few steps around the corner from a wet lab where David worked. Since she chatted with him from time to time, Trish felt no hesitation with stopping by. David was working with the HPLC unit and looking unhappy.

"Problems?"

"Oh, hello, Dr. Trish. Yes, this instrument is being cranky today. Must have a bad spirit in it."

"You don't believe that, do you?"

"No," he laughed. "It seems to have a mind of its own sometimes. Think I'll give up on it for now and try again tomorrow."

"It's coffee time. Are you going down for some?" "Sure.

Want to join me?" David smiled and said, "Let me get Trahn in the next lab. We usually go together. You're welcome to join us." The Coffee Shop on the ground floor of the Medical School was Trish's preferred spot to eat in the Medical Center, without the hustle of the main Cafeteria or the Deli. Few hospital staff, patients, or their families used it, because it was a five-minute walk.

"So, what's new with you, Dr. Trish?" asked David as he sipped a Starbucks' concoction slathered with whipped cream and Trish added skim milk to her decaf cup of java.

"Oh, the usual: kids, husband, and work. And you?"

"The lab's going great; especially with the new grant money. We should have enough data to crunch some numbers in another month or so. Everyone's been preoccupied with Mi Ling's death."

"You knew her?"

"Sure, Su is a friend, too. Poor guy, he is really broken up over her death. Says he can't keep his mind on his work."

"Had she been ill lately? Under the weather?" "Here comes Su. He can tell you more. Hi, man, join us."

"Dr. Trish, Su Quan. Su, Dr. McLeod. Call her Dr. Trish."

"Hello, nice to meet you. Wish it was under better circumstances," replied Su.

"So sorry to hear of your fiancée's death, Su. Did you know I was the one who discovered her body?"

"The police detective who questioned me told me."

"How did that go? The questioning, that is."

"Okay, I guess. I don't want to ruffle any feathers, as you say here. After all, I'm on a student visa, but that fellow wasn't polite."

"Did you catch his name?"

"He introduced himself so short, I didn't catch his name, but he had a badge. Said 'Detective Bill Swanson?' Acted as if someone had killed her and it might be me. He even acted surprised that we weren't living together if we were engaged.

Asked me why not. At home in our family, that would not happen. We're a Christian family."

"And you're from China?"

"Yes, our family converted many years ago, back in the 1920's when missionaries came to our city. My uncles and father suffered much during the Cultural Revolution under Mao. Father was a chemist and was assigned to work on a pig farm where he cleaned the pens. It was an extremely difficult and trying time; a real test of my father's faith. I was just a boy."

"What kind of visa did Mi Ling have?"

"She was on a student visa. We hoped to get green cards and to become citizens."

"Now that she's gone, do you think you'll stay?"

"Yes. I love my family, but have many friends here. The weather and atmosphere here on the coast is similar in many ways to back home. No, God willing, this is my home and country now. I would like to go to graduate school and continue in the area of research that Mi Ling was working on."

"What was that?" "Her research was in the cardiovascular area. She had some terrific ideas and was told her work had great potential."

"I hate to sound so inquisitive as you are probably still in somewhat of a state of shock, but how had her health been?"

"Extremely good. She wasn't one to even have a cold or the sniffles; however, she had complained of feeling tired and fatigued over the past few months."

"How so?"

"I told her she wasn't getting enough rest, but she said she didn't need much sleep and was excited about her work."

"Did she come in to the lab on weekends or late at night?"

"Weekends, yes; on Saturdays. Sundays, we went to church together. Nights, no, never after 5:30 or 6:00 pm."

"Tell me more about that."

"You remember the Chinese graduate student who was

raped and murdered a few years back? David told me about that."

"Oh, God, yes. It was horrid. I was at the Mental Health Clinic that morning, and Clyde came to my office and related that a body was found."

"Mi Ling didn't know her, but heard all about it when she arrived. The girl was in many ways like her: bright, kind, and so excited about, in her case, school and her graduate research. The man who did it was a construction worker on the research tower who had access at night to the school. It wasn't clear if she was dead or not when he threw her off the tenth floor of the tower. She landed over there, just outside this very atrium," Su said, pointing with his hand. "By the time Mi Ling came as a postdoctoral fellow, there was much more in the way of security."

"Seems I remember the guy was on video and that was how he was apprehended," said Trish.

"That's right. He even had a wife and two young children. He got life without parole. They should have pulled out the electric chair," said David. "The way things go around here, in fifteen years, the Governor will give him a pardon."

"I certainly hope not," replied Trish. "That was a risk management nightmare. I bet the higher-ups in administration were quaking in their boots when the grieving parents came all the way from China. Ever think how difficult it was to take her body back to China. Sorry, Su. What about Mi Ling?"

"She was buried here. We have friends in a small country church and they arranged for her to be placed in the cemetery next to the church."

"It's a damn shame," David said. "There had to be a murder for the security system to be upgraded those years ago; but if you ask me, a bunch of video cameras isn't adequate for prevention. They get to see the crimes when in view of a camera. For Mi Ling that would not helped. There aren't any cameras near that location."

"Su, do you have any idea why she would have gone into the stairwell?" asked Trish.

"She did spend time in the library, and frequently after supper for a while, especially if she ate here at the Medical Center. It didn't get dark until late and she might have gone there for a breath of air, but not this time of year. It's too hot in there."

"We really need to not discuss this further now. You've been through enough, Su. My heart goes out to you. I'll ask my church friends to remember you in prayer."

"Thanks, Dr. Trish. That means a lot to me."

"Sorry to cut this off," David said, "but I need to get back to my infernal HPLC. I'd swear it has a bad spirit in it today. Oh, not really, but I do have some samples to run."

"Me, too. I enjoyed visiting with you young guys, even if circumstances could have been better."

"Thanks, nice to meet you, Dr. Trish. David had told me good things about you."

❋

TWENTY-FOUR

Several weeks later when the Lunch Bunch group met at Clare's house with Trish, Helen and Barb B, were ready for a chick chat. The main topic of conversation was Mi Ling's death.

"It's lovely we meet once a month," said Helen, "However, after Hilda's murder was solved, I didn't think we'd be discussing murder again."

"This time we don't even know if it is murder for sure," replied Trish. "I have this funny feeling something isn't right, even if the police are involved and the post said cardiac arrest probably secondary to an arrhythmia. The facts are not congruent."

"Young people do die from that. Look at that basketball player who dropped on the court last year in New Orleans. The only reason some athletes survive an attack is immediate medical attention. If she was alone, no one would know," noted Clare.

"But why go into a hot stairwell, or at least a warm one? The library is air-conditioned. Her fiancé did tell me that she had been tired and fatigued over the past month or two, a change for her. He thought it was just overwork."

"Did you ask him about the blue heart tattoo?" asked Helen.

"Not directly. I asked David later. I felt a little uncomfortable pumping Su, since her death is considered from natural causes. David said she had it when she came over from Hong Kong. As a teenager, she was in some sort of Society and they all had one somewhere on their bodies. She never talked about it, except to say when she had saved enough money, she planned to have laser treatments to remove it."

Clare chimed in, "Trish, you say she was experiencing fatigue? Did anyone check for Hepatitis C or B? Sometimes that is contracted from a tattoo and doesn't show up for several years. She could be fatigued from that."

"Could you check on that from your sources?"

"Sure. I doubt if they ran that test, but I'm sure they kept specimens and samples."

"But why are you so curious? What makes you suspicious about the cause of death and suspect other than a natural cause?" countered Clare.

"Okay, girls, I have something to show ya'll." Trish produced the two notes.

"MIND YOUR OWN BUSINESS?" Helen read the notes. "What's this about?"

"Hell if I know," said Trish, "but I don't like it. My curiosity about Mi Ling is the only thing I have done out of the ordinary."

"You did check out the heart tattoo at the tattoo studio," said Clare.

"Maybe we should talk to that girl I saw in the grocery line who had a blue heart tattoo," said Helen.

"There is a total of five people we know about with a blue heart tattoo. The man on the beach, Mi Ling, the gal in Winn-Dixie, and two volunteers that came through the Psychopharm Research Unit," continued Trish.

"All were Asian," added Helen

"And two are now dead," remarked Barb.

"Trish thinks Mi Ling's might not be natural, and no one would classify a bullet hole in the back of the head as natural or accidental," continued Helen.

"The volunteer for the Psychopharm study that didn't qualify and the one you saw. They should be around and not dead," said Clare.

"To be sure. I forgot about her. She's alive as far as I know."

"Do you think we should try and talk to her?" "Why not?"

"You take the gal you saw at Winn-Dixie, Helen."

"Me? How would I do that?" said Helen, her eyes wide.

"Do you remember the day and time you saw her?" "Yes, I think so."

"So, go to the grocery that day and at that time for a little while. Maybe you'll see her again. Strike up a conversation. You're good at that."

"Oh," sighed Helen.

"And do you know one particular cashier?" "Sure. It's Adele most every time. She's such a sweetheart. I'll ask her if she knows her name. If she used a credit card, her name would be on the ticket," continued Helen.

"Now you're cooking with Crisco, girl!"

"And," said Barb, "even if she didn't remember, she could check for it next time she comes through her line."

"Now, what about the Psychopharm reject? I was the one who noticed it," said Trish. "Somehow, I don't think I should contact her, and I don't know who the earlier volunteer was with the tattoo."

"We have her name and address and phone number," said Clare. "Maybe there's a way I can contact her and find out where she works, or if she goes to a gym, or to a particular fast food place."

"Crafty Clare at work again," laughed Barb.

"This curiosity bug is contagious, and Trish is infecting all of us. I must admit, the tattoo is a puzzle, even if it has nothing to do with Mi Ling's death. Especially so when you consider it might not be a heart if viewed from another angle," continued Barb.

"And, there is something about the fact that Mi Ling planned on having hers removed and that she got it while she was in Hong Kong, China. Also, she didn't tell her fiancé much about why she had it," said Trish.

"I think we should ask her roommates what they know."

"Great! That can be your job."

"Sorry I brought it up."

"No, that's something you can do. Find out if they are dating any other male students. Lean on them. Bat your eyes."

"Really! An old broad like me, in a white coat, batting my eyes!"

"Okay, put on eye make-up first."

Barb laughed. "You're a real case."

"I know. Isn't it fun? I hope I am not being too bossy with you all."

TWENTY-FIVE

"What have you been doing, checking out the chicks on the dock?" asked Trish, as Steven came up behind her in the kitchen and kissed her on the neck. "Not bad, but not as good as you, and I hooked a couple of nice lemons – fish, not chicks, that is."

"Great, I'll cook them. Lemon fish are good eating."

"Puffer fish were bad today. The guys must have caught seven or eight of those suckers."

"Did ya'll throw them back?"

"Not today. We usually do, but Dan said some stupid little man had been hanging around and paying a dollar a piece for them."

"No way! Those things are poison. I learned that when I was a little kid. Only thing good is they are cute when they are puffed up, dried and lacquered; makes a nice decoration for a beach house."

"I don't know what this guy was buying them for, but Dan said he'd been hanging around several months, asking if anyone caught any, and buying them, so Dan stopped throwing them back."

"That's curious. I did read that in Japan, if they are dressed out properly and the poison parts — skin, guts, gonads, etc. — are removed, they are said to make wonderful sushi. Did you consider asking him? Or did he look like some poor demented soul?"

"We were in a rush, and truthfully, it didn't cross my mind.

The next time I see him, I'll ask for you, Ms. Doctor 'Curious as a Cat.'" Steven grinned at Trish and blew her a kiss.

"Now, Steven. It is true I'm a curious person, and that has served me well, both in conducting psychotherapy as well as research at the Medical Center. Did I tell you the heart-shaped tattoo the cop saw on the body at the beach and the one I saw on Mi Ling at school may not be a heart after all?"

"No, you didn't, but what of it?"

"It may have only been the angle I was looking from. If you look at it another way, it looks like antlers or horns. I had coffee a couple of days ago with David from the department, and David told me she was planning on having laser surgery to remove it as soon as she had saved enough money."

"So why was she planning on that?"

"Somehow, I got the idea it had to do with her becoming a Christian and the tattoo was a mark of something she had grown beyond."

"That sounds reasonable to me; it's like a gang member who no longer wants to be identified by a tattoo."

"Her fiancé said she had good health, but had complained of feeling fatigued over the past couple of months. He thought she was stressed out from her work in the library and lab. We — that is my Lunch Bunch girl friends — are going to talk to another woman we've seen with the same tattoo There was a woman Helen saw at Winn-Dixie, and I think we can locate the research volunteer who I noticed had that blue heart tattoo."

"I hope you ladies aren't getting into something as you did a couple of years ago with the body you saw at the Mental Health Clinic."

"The police aren't even investigating any deaths this time even though the man at the beach had a bullet in his brain. The sheriff — not the police — are responsible for that fellow. We're simply checking out a few things."

"What about those two notes you received, Trish? I don't like it. They seem like a threat of some sort."

"I'll admit, I feel a little uncomfortable about them myself. Play with the kids a few minutes while I finish supper, will ya?"

Trish rewashed the lemon fish, zip bagged them and stored them in the freezer. *Why would someone want puffer fish? I think I'll bounce that off Barb tomorrow at school. She, being a toxicologist, may have some ideas.*

❉

TWENTY-SIX

"The Chairman has called a faculty meeting today, noon in the big seminar room," said Sheila as Trish took the mail from her box.

"I'm sure there's an e-mail from him. However, any idea what it's about?"

"Not a clue."

"I was hoping with this Chairman, we would only meet once a month. At least, that's what he said when he came. A person can get meeting'd out around this place. They probably have a meeting to tell housekeeping which way to make the rolls of toilet paper go in the restrooms."

"You're right about that. A great deal of what I put in faculty boxes is notification of some committee meeting or task force. I thought when we got e-mail in place that would lessen the paper notes, but hell, there are bunches of idiots who don't check their e-mail."

"To change the subject, ever hear of a place that serves sushi around here?"

"No, I think there's at least one spot over in Louisiana that does. You wanting to eat some?"

"No way, raw fish, ugh."

"It's not all raw fish but I think most is."

Back in her office, Trish called Martha, "Is he serving us lunch?"

"Of course, Dr. Trish, need you ask? Today it will be the lunch special from the hospital cafeteria: meatloaf, mashed garlic potatoes, seasoned green beans, rolls and brownies."

"How unhealthy, and this place is a Medical Center. Those green beans swim in fatback. I'll get a veggie wrap from the deli."

"You're a good example for the rest of us. Wish I could do like you." Martha fought the battle of the bulge and in spite of a few successful skirmishes from time to time, had decided it was a lost cause for her.

It was 11:45; veggie wrap in hand, when Trish took her usual spot at the long table in the seminar room, saving an adjacent seat for Clare. Barb Bonno always sat with the other Ph.D.s. It was interesting how the group sorted themselves out, even within each group, with full professors sitting near the head of the table and instructors and assistant professors at the foot; except Trish and Clare refused to sit near the head. As Clare slipped into her chair, Trish whispered, "Chairmen come and go and we endure, do we not?"

"You can say that again. Know what this is about?"

"Nope."

The meeting turned out to be rather bland. The business manager had complained of some late billing slips and inadequate coding. As usual, some faculty seemed to disappear during the day and were not available for emergencies.

Trish whispered to Clare, "He should know by now that supervising psychiatrists and psychologists is like herding cats."

"That's exactly why I'm happy with the Consultation-Liaison service. Even at that, I have more administrative junk to do than I want," replied Clare, as they exited the meeting.

"Me, too. I like this Chair a little better than some we've had in the past, but he is still a loser in my book. His main drawback is he's too chummy with the Weasel, Wesley Weaver."

"Oh, I wasn't aware of that."

"Yep. Unfortunately, they frequently eat lunch together. Must feed on each other's narcissism. Rumor is, the Weasel Leprechaun is going to get an endowed chair. So, maybe our leprechaun Parker wants to get in line for an endowed chair ditto."

"There's no doubt about it. I hate it. How Parker slaps his name on every paper the Ph.D.'s put out, when most of the time, he doesn't do a damn thing on their projects."

"I hear the weasel Leprechaun Weaver is the same. Stands on the shoulders of his grad students and postdoc fellows. Remember, Mi Ling was under him."

"Did he treat her well?"

"From what I hear, she was such a sweetheart. No complaint would ever pass her lips, even if he didn't. From what David says, she was a person of high moral character and would never do anything dishonest or illegal. Very few, if any, lacunea in her superego."

❁

"Trish, I have some more information regarding Mi Ling," said Clare as they entered Trish's office and closed the door.

"Great! What is it?"

"The student worker in the library from the night before she died remembered Mi Ling. She came in the main entrance just before five and past his workstation at the checkout desk. He never saw her leave by that entrance. He also told me she was a frequent patron, three or four nights a week; had her own special nook she used on the second floor back in the stacks. That's where her purse, a shawl, and papers were found."

"It does get chilly back there."

"And guess what she was reading up on?"

"I haven't a clue. Tell me."

"It was a strange assortment of articles on the eastern salamander, toads, blue-ring octopus, and puffer fish. Also, something dealing with a new assay for tetrodotoxin."

"Tetrodotoxin! Wow! That's one of the most potent poisons anywhere. Every year, there are a couple of deaths in

California from eating sushi made from improperly prepared puffer fish."

"And, listen to this. None of those articles have even the remotest relationship to her research in Weaver's lab."

"So, why was she researching it?" "Beats me, but she sure was looking into it."

"Do you think someone could come in the library and not be noticed by the student at the front desk?" "Yes, I do. Many's the time I had to hunt one up to check out a book or journal."

"Was there anything else found in her study nook?" "Only a box that had the remains of a salad. There isn't supposed to be any food in the library. Apparently, she broke that rule."

"So, as we know, we all have superego lacunea, and breaking that rule was one of hers."

"Maybe she didn't bring the food into the library. Maybe someone else did."

"It's time for me to read up on tetrodotoxin."

"Why?"

"Just a hunch, a tickle at the base of my brain, if you will. And, we need a Lunch Bunch meeting soon. I'll call Helen if you'll call Barb."

"Sure. When?"

"My house, this Saturday, 11:00 a.m."

❋

TWENTY-SEVEN

"Welcome. Come on in, and take a load off your minds," said Trish, as she greeted her trio of friends.

"We have the house to ourselves, except for Smoke and Skip. Steven took the kids fishing."

"Isn't Amy too little for that?"

"No. She just watches them and loves it."

Skip bounded from woman to woman for attention, dancing on his feet, not daring to put a paw on anyone.

"He'll calm down after ya'll give him a hug. Let's go in the family room," said Trish as she led the way.

"Damn, aren't we a case?"

"What are you talking about?"

"Look at us. Everyone of us is sitting in the same place we always do."

"Okay," said Barb, "let's do fruit basket turnover and switch." And they all had switched seats when Trish re-entered the room with a tray of glasses and a pitcher of iced tea.

"What's this? You're all sitting in different chairs."

"We've decided to stimulate our brains by not being set in our ways."

"If it works, I'll not knock it. Here, I'll change chairs, too."

"So, what's new?" started Clare, almost as if they were a therapy group.

"Not much on the home front. Reggie is still sober. I was worried for a while there he had fallen off the wagon. He's been fishing a lot more. Says it helps."

"That's good news. Did you ask Adele about the girl you saw at Winn-Dixie with the tattoo?"

"Sure did. And, she gave me her name and where she worked."

"That's cool. Did you go on by?" "Yes, but that's where things went bad."

"Went bad? What do you mean?" "She worked in a beauty supply shop, so I pretended I needed some items."

"Hair color, I bet," said Clare.

"Okay, so it was hair color. It's no secret that I tint my hair. Anyway, when I asked if Monica was around, the girl behind the counter told me that she had died."

"Died?" gasped Barb.

"You've got to be kidding!"

"I'm not, I swear. So, I asked her how. All she said was that it was very sudden. They didn't even get her to the hospital. Told her mama her tongue was tingling and she couldn't breathe. She fell down in a 'fit' and by the time the medics arrived, she was dead."

"How long was that?" asked Trish.

"That was another concern. It took them thirty minutes after 911 was called. The emergency crew couldn't find the house. It was back on a dead-end street and the call was made on a cell phone. Her poor mama didn't speak English too well."

"Oh, my God," exclaimed Trish. "Was this young woman Asian?"

"She didn't look much that way to me in the grocery, but the girl in the beauty supply shop said she was from some place in Southeast Asia. Her mama had married a service man and come to the States."

"You sure got a lot of information."

"People just like to tell me things. Really, ya'll, I didn't pump the beauty supply girl. She seemed to need to talk, so I let her."

"Did you buy anything?"

"Of course. They had my color of tint, but that had nothing to do with the information she gave."

"You didn't happen to get her mama's name or address did you?"

"Why, yes, I did."

"Damnation! Bless my butt, we're going to rename you Shirlenelock."

"I was just doing what I thought you wanted me to."

"Sure, sweetheart. Did you go see her mama?"

"It wasn't much out of my way, on a sandwich run. I haven't been doing many myself since the business has expanded so, but one of my drivers was sick, so-o-o…"

"So, don't keep us in suspense."

"It was sorta sad. Just a little frame house — almost a shack — up on piers. I gave her three of my leftover sandwiches."

"Jesus! I can't believe, in this day and time, you just walked up to a stranger's house; much less, she let you inside. What lie did you make up?"

"Only a little one. I said I had heard from her co-worker that her daughter had died and our church did outreach to grieving families."

"It doesn't."

"I know, but it could. Anyway, she let me in and we had a nice chat and I prayed with her."

"Prayed with her?"

"She looked like she needed it, and thanked me. She's now caring for her grandbaby. The husband is at sea on a freighter. Won't be back for several months."

"What else did you find out?" asked Clare.

"They had eaten lunch and about an hour later, her daughter had complained of her tongue tingling; said she couldn't breathe and fell over."

"What did they eat for lunch?"

"I did have sense enough to ask that. The old lady said

some kind of soup like sweet and sour, rice and a few boiled shrimp. But, she ate the same thing and she didn't get sick."

"There must be more, I suppose. The coroner did an autopsy. Did you ask her?"

"She said, yes, and she was buried a week ago. They were Christians — Baptist to boot."

"Okay. Boy, my curiosity button has really been punched now. Say, Barb, could you see what the post showed?"

"I think you should. You know McInnis better than I do."

"You're right. I'll give him a call. Now, girls, this is the second woman — both young — who has died recently and they both had the same tattoo. I think that's more than a coincidence. Helen, did the mama say what the young woman did after she ate lunch before she collapsed?"

"She did leave the house briefly; walked down to where a little dock is behind the house- a bayou of sorts — shallow, but deep enough for a flat bottom skiff. She wasn't gone but ten or fifteen minutes."

"Could she have met someone there?"

"Her mother didn't know. The girl didn't say anything. She had been worried about finances, with her husband gone, the baby and all."

"This may have nothing to do with what we're chatting about, but, did you come up with any ideas why someone would be paying money for puffer fish?"

"Not really. Some places, they do eat them, but that's taking a risk. Some appear to be loaded with poison tetrodotoxin to be exact. It's concentrated in the gut and gonads mostly, but could be some in the skin. Not every blowfish is toxic, though. Did any of you all hear of anyone making homemade sushi around here?"

"No," they all replied.

"I find it difficult to believe some little man was blowing them up and drying them to sell as souvenirs. There's quite a bit of research being done using tetrodotoxin. I'm not sure anyone in our school is though."

"That fits with the little I dug up," Barb continued. "Some research is being done in pain and cardiac areas. The poison acts on sodium ion channels, but anyone doing research would just order it from a supply house. Mi Ling may have had an idea for a research project. My references said the discovery of the guanidine moiety on tetrodotoxin molecule was part of why Woodward received a Nobel Prize in Chemistry back in the eighties. So, who knows what ideas she had. If she were murdered, would that be enough to be a motive?" sighed Trish as she frowned.

"It wouldn't be the first time. Jealousy is a powerful thing," said Clare. "Which reminds me of my assignment, if you will. I checked on the psychopharm reject. No answer on the phone. It's been disconnected. I even stopped by the address. It wasn't far from the Medical Center — a four-plex with two spaces downstairs and two up. Spoke to a guy in the drive who was working on his car. He never heard of her. Said he knew everyone who lived there, he'd lived there for four years himself, so that's a dead end."

"Did she get any money for coming to your research unit?" asked Helen.

"I think we paid her twenty-five dollars, and it's not unusual for volunteers to lie about addresses and phone numbers; just another way for a free handout. Fortunately, they aren't that common."

"So, this is a dead end, eh?" said Helen.

"Does look that way, but where is she, and what is she doing? Could she have been Monica?"

Barb put in at that point, "I found out the routine tox studies were negative on Mi Ling, and she didn't have Hepatitis C or B."

"Wouldn't it be something if she died from tetrodotoxin? That wouldn't show up on your usual tox study," chirped Clare.

Barb replied, "There are some new unapproved assays that

show it. I might be able to squirrel around and get someone to run them if ya'll think it worth the effort."

"I sure do. However, I need to bounce this off McInnis first. I'll get back to you on that," said Trish.

"No problem. This is a time I can pull in payback around the school. I've done favors for years, so it'll be tit-for-tat if you think it's needed."

"Oh, my God, it's a quarter to twelve. I've got to go!"

"Time flies when you're having fun."

"It sure has this morning."

"You had some good things to report, Barb. And you, too, Clare."

"Get back to us after you talk to McInnis."

"Will do, and if we decide to ask for the tetrodotoxin assay, let's wait until that's back before we meet again. Is that okay with ya'll?"

"Sure thing," the trio replied in unison.

"My house, next time," said Clare, as they exited the front door to see Steven drive up.

TWENTY-EIGHT

It was Sunday night after the babies were in bed, before Trish called Burt McInnis, the Coroner.

"Hi, this is Trish, your friendly pest. How's tricks?" "Oh, hi, Trish. Everything as good as it can be with limited funds, and by the way, you're never a pest. Hilda Rasberry's murder would never have been solved without your curiosity. What are you curious about now?"

"Remember the young woman I discovered in the stairwell at the Medical School?"

"Sure, I let the guys there do the post. I have more than enough work."

"Do you know the results?" "Nothing unusual. Looked like a cardiac arrhythmia and no one nearby to aid her."

"Could she have been poisoned?"

"Anything's possible. Nothing showed up on the tox studies. She had a little non-specific internal bleeding. What are you thinking?"

"Tetrodotoxin."

"I don't see how. There was no indication she had eaten any fish. Appeared to be, as best I remember, salad fragments in the gastric contents."

"What if someone got her to go into the stairwell to chat or for a breath of air or to warm up? It was chilly from the air conditioning back in her study nook."

"I suppose anything is possible. There have been deaths within 20-30 minutes of ingestion of contaminated fish. We usually make the diagnosis based on history of eating fish or sushi. If the patient lives to make it to Emergency Services and we can give life support and keep them alive another 24 hours, recovery is complete without sequela."

"What if she were given it in some form other than fish?"

"That would be hard to detect. There are some unapproved assays using HPLC in tandem with mass spectrometry that researchers in Japan say can detect it in mouse serum."

"The pathologist at school must have stored specimens and blood?"

"Sure."

"Burt, I just have this tickle in my brain that poison has something to do with her death. Did you know what she was reading in her study space?"

"Can't say I do."

"She had articles on the eastern salamander, puffer fish (otherwise known as blowfish,) blue-ringed octopus, plus some other similar critters. And what do these animals have in common?"

"They all can contain tetrodotoxin. Usually in the gonads."

"Point made. And my toxicologist friend tells me that consciousness remains until death. The victim can't move or hardly breathe, but they can hear and see. It's similar to the effects of zombie powder used in Haiti."

"My God, what a horrible, sadistic way to kill someone. The victim is helpless, but conscious until the moment of death. I think it's a stretch to say who killed Mi Ling — wasn't that her name? — because articles on it were found in her study area."

"I've asked Barb to pull in payback for favors she's done over the years and ask to have the unapproved assay run. Maybe you could help by talking to our path guys to release the necessary serum."

"I'd be glad to."

"Even if that proved to be the case, we still have no inkling as to the who or why of murder."

"I'll call Sonja in Clinical Path tomorrow. She followed

me a couple of years in residency. Have Dr. Bonno contact her in a few days."

"Will do. Stay in touch."

❀

TWENTY-NINE

As Trish replaced the phone, she thought *Crap, I forgot to ask about Monica's post. Bet he did it. I'll ask him the next time I talk to him.*

"Going to stay up all night, Trish? Remember, tomorrow's Monday."

"Be there in a shake. Need to turn on the dishwasher and check Smoke's food. He's such a night eater."

It was near eleven after cozy, gentle lovemaking, when Trish remembered the little man buying puffer fish.

"Did you ever find out anything more why that fellow was buying puffer fish?"

"Unnh, yeah, ask me in the morning, I'm near sleep now."

"Okay, lover; you deserve a good night's sleep. Sweet dreams."

Trish turned on her side and began to drift into sleep, but this night it didn't come quickly as it always did after orgasmic lovemaking. *What's wrong with me? Thinking about murder and death when I've just had a lovely intimate time with Steven. Sometimes I wish I wasn't so curious or observant. Okay, God, I give up. It's the way you made me.* At this thought, she experienced a release and drifted quickly into sleep, not to awaken until six the next morning when Smoke jumped into the bed and began to paw-stomp her back, purring loudly.

"I'm up. I'm up, Smoke," said Trish as she went to check on the kids. They were still sound asleep. The automatic timer had already made coffee for Steven, and she was having a cup of mint, decaf green tea when Steven came to the breakfast table. Kissing her on the head, he smiled and said, "Good sleep, good dreams."

"Don't remember last night's dreams, but I am refreshed. You?"

"The same. About that question you asked, the fellow that was buying puffer fish?"

"Yes, what did you find out?"

"I asked John, and he did a little investigating, if you will. It seems rather mysterious. The fellow puts them in a cooler on ice. Leaves the cooler on his back porch and tells the owner of the oriental market he has some. Sometime during the night, some unknown person picks up the cooler and leaves another in its place with a Ziploc plastic bag inside containing the money — one dollar each. The fellow at the oriental market doesn't get them. He wasn't sure even of the woman's name who offered the money, just that she had a British accent and said they were for research at the Medical Center."

"Medical Center? Wow!"

"John didn't say for sure, but at least fifty or sixty fish total. But he's not bringing them anymore."

"Thanks. I'll ask around school."

"Course, that could be a lie, too. Gotta run."

"See you tonight."

It was a short thirty minutes later when Mercedes arrived just as Adam toddled out of his room.

"How's my boy? Sleep good?"

Adam then ran for a hug from Trish and said, "Work."

"Sure thing, Champ. Here's your Mercedes." Adam broke into a smile as Mercedes entered the kitchen.

"Listen to a few things on the tape I need you to do today. Have a good day," said Trish as she gathered her purse, briefcase, and tote bag.

As she drove to the Medical School, Trish's mind drifted

to the death of Mi Ling and the information that someone at the Medical School might be doing something with puffer fish. *But, if a person was doing research, why get a bunch of fish? Why not order it from the supply house? Unless they didn't want anyone to know they had any tetrodotoxin.*

THIRTY

"Can you take a break?" It was mid-week when Barb Bonno stopped by Trish's office.

"Sure, I'm finished on yet another PowerPoint presentation. What's up?"

"Listen, I can get the serum run to check for tetrodotoxin. Also talked to the gal, but McInnis called in Clinical Path, and she can get the serum for us."

"Barb, I forgot to ask McInnis what the autopsy showed on Monica, the gal Helen saw in the checkout line who died, but I will, and I'll bet he will give us some serum from her."

"That's a good idea. Remember, her mama said her tongue was tingling and that's an early sign of that type of poisoning. How she got it is a mystery."

"Heck, let's call McInnis right now." Trish quickly punched in the Coroner's Office number.

"Hello, good afternoon. Would you ask if Dr. McInnis is available for a call from Dr. Trish McLeod?"

Aside to Barb, Trish whispered, "I hate to pull the 'doctor' bit, but sometimes it does make it easier to get through to people like Burt."

"Oh, hi, Burt. Trish here. Say, we're going to be able to run the assay on Mi Ling's serum. By the way, did you do the post on an Asian or part-Asian young woman, Monica something? You did? Mind telling me if you found anything suspicious? I'm just getting obsessed about tetrodotoxin. What her mother described to my friend, Helen, is consistent with that type of poisoning, except she hadn't eaten any fish."

"Got a second, Trish? I've got that file right here. Nothing very specific on hers, either. Tox studies negative, internal bleeding, probable cardiac arrhythmia leading to respiratory arrest. This is interesting. Gastric contents showed vegetable fragments, salad greens."

"Her mother didn't say she had eaten any salad. I know I'm grasping, but would you mind supplying some serum, and since Barb Bonno has gone to the trouble to run the assay on Mi Ling's, we might as well on Felicia's."

"That's okay by me. If it should be possible, we have no idea of a motive or suspect, do we?"

"The only connection between the two women is they both had a blue heart tattoo and were Asian, as far as we know."

"Let me know the results and then we can think about talking to the authorities."

"Will do. Catch you later."

As Trish replaced the receiver, she said to Barb, "You said someone in the school was using tetrodotoxin in pain research?"

"Yes, Bonté in Anesthesiology."

"Ask him to check his supply and be sure none is missing, will you?"

THIRTY-ONE

It was several weeks later when the Lunch Bunch of hen medics plus Helen, met at Clare's house.

"Sorry we had to skip a couple of weeks. I forgot I had backup call last weekend. And, let me tell ya'll, it was a weekend from hell," said Clare.

"I've had a couple of those myself. Was it the usual? Too many patients, not enough beds and a resident less than astute? I lucked out the weekend before — only six admits in the entire weekend."

"The luck of the draw as I see it. Every time I think I've seen everything, something new comes down the block. The only saving grace this weekend was that we had two terrific medical students; one who printed as fast as I can type. We had an addict who had injected Lysol intravenously for a high. Boy, did he get psychotic! Took several hours to calm him and when I asked why he did it, he only said "It was all I could find." And a hostile bastard to boot. I won't see him again until he comes in to die on Medicine and we get a psych consultation request."

"Then he'll be so pitiful, your heart will go out to him," said Trish.

"Unfortunately, that's all too common, but at least I can show and feel a little compassion for the poor souls then. It's hard to do that when they act the way this jerk did on Saturday night and I was in the middle of controlling him."

"Don't worry, Helen, honey," said Barb. "They don't go through this every month. They share the faculty call and if they happen to be assigned to the inpatient unit, it's almost totally by phone after rounds are finished with the resident."

"Makes my world a mite tame by comparison," said Helen.

"Oh, you've told us of some ups and downs yourself. What you deal with isn't less, just different. Like apples and oranges."

"Maybe so. Which reminds me, did you talk to any of Mi Ling's apartment mates?" asked Helen.

"For sure, and you all will be surprised what she said. I only talked to one girl. She and two others shared their two-bedroom apartment. Dr. Weasel had the hots for Mi Ling," said Barb.

"You're kidding! He's a horse's ass, but with his postdoc?"

"Yes. I know he has that sweet wife, who, by the way, works in our library."

"Sudra — that's the roommate, said whenever they met alone, he said very suggestive things."

"Such as?"

"The usual — how he found Asian women exciting and mysterious and how lovely he bet her body was. About two weeks before she died, Mi Ling confided to Sudra that he was holding her hand and patting her on her tush."

"Did anyone else ever see anything?" asked Trish.

"I asked her, or rather, told her we had policies in place to handle sexual harassment, and she said they didn't know how or who to tell. Mi Ling thought the best thing was to avoid being alone with him," replied Barb.

"Did he ever threaten her?" chimed in Helen.

"Not in the usual sense, but he did in regard to her research ideas and how much power he had because of his connections. He implied he could stymie her career opportunities for grants, faculty appointments, and the like.

"She didn't tell her fiancé, either. She feared he would do something rash. Sudra said she just wanted to finish the data collection, publish, and then relocate far from Dr. Weaver. And, to boot, the Weasel had informed her he would be listed as first author. That sure wasn't fair. The hypothesis was brilliant and her methodology very tight."

"So, why wouldn't Dr. Weaver give her credit?" asked Helen.

"Cause he's a turd," quipped Trish. "Actually, he, in my book, is jealous as hell; bucking for an endowed chair, and scuttlebutt is he may be nominated the next time around."

"Why would he be enamored of her if he was so jealous?" said Helen.

"Probably comes down to the same ol' control issues. He's that way for sure. Even rolls over into committee meetings he's on. Would the Weasel have any tetrodotoxin in his lab?"

"I suppose anything's possible, but my sources say not. He has a couple of techs in his labs, but there's a big turnover there; they never stay more than a year. He's apparently a tyrant."

"Barb, you've been a busy beaver. What about the assays for tetrodotoxin?"

"By damn! I forgot to tell ya'll. They were both positive. The information was turned over to McInnis and he told the police."

"Whoa," said Trish, "They're sure?"

"Yes, both Mi Ling and Felicia, the gal Helen saw at the grocery."

"How did they get the poison?"

"That's a mystery. Neither one had eaten anything and that is the usual source," said Barb.

"So, foul play?"

"Looks that way to me."

"Did Bonte' say if any of his was missing from the safe in his lab," ask Trish?

"I asked and he said "No," replied Barb.

"I think I'll put a bug in whoever the detective's ear is on that case," said Trish.

"Tomorrow is my day to supervise students at the Mental Health Clinic and I'll see ol' Clyde. He's sure to know if

Swanson is or will be assigned to the case once the police know it is a possible homicide."

"Clyde still goes to Mental Health even after his promotion?"

"Yes. He says he likes the extra money, and he's been doing it so long, he knows most of the patients and enjoys chatting with them. He still credits us in solving Hilda Rasberry's death and his resultant promotion to Sergeant."

THIRTY-TWO

"Bless my soul, if it ain't the lovely Dr. Trish." Clyde was standing by the chrome entry gate adjacent to the first floor reception window.

"Hi, Clyde. Haven't seen you in a while. How're you doing these days?"

"Couldn't be better. Susie, is ever thankful you got her connected with Ms. Helen. They have quite a nice little sandwich catering business."

"Helen couldn't have done it without Susie. Got a minute? Ride up on the elevator with me. I have a question to ask you."

As they entered the elevator and the door closed, Clyde said, "You cain't stop doing more of that messing into crime can you, Dr. Trish? I be thinking all that over Ms. Hilda's death would satisfy a body 'long those lines."

"You know me — always curious. And I told you I was the one who found the body of the young woman at the Medical School."

"Yep, sure did. Hope that didn't set off the curiosity button of yours too strong."

"It has in a way. Come in my office for a few minutes and I'll bring you up to date."

Trish quickly related the events she and her friends had discussed.

"So now, Clyde, do you know who is working those cases?"

"Bill Swanson checked on the one at the Medical School, but since the autopsy didn't show anything out of the ordinary, it wasn't considered homicide; and the other lady, the same. Don't think these were connected, do you?"

"It's another mystery. Both women were Asian, and both had a blue heart tattooed on their necks, and now we know both were poisoned."

"Poisoned? How'd that be missed? How'd ya'll come to that?"

"The one at the Medical School had been reading about a poison that's in puffer fish, and Dr. Barb arranged for a special unapproved assay to be run on their serum and both had it. So, my friend, Burt McInnis, the coroner, told the authorities."

"That will mean Swanson will be back on the cases. He'll want to talk to you for sure."

"He already did, right after I found Mi Ling's body."

"I'll keep my ears open and let you know anything I hear, but don't you think it best to leave this kind of work to us?"

"Of course, but, as usual, I'm obsessing about these deaths, as are my three friends. And, you must admit, Hilda's killer would never have been caught if it weren't for us. See if you can find anything out about a blue heart symbol? They both were well done; not the usual seen on gang member. Those look rough round the edges."

Two students appeared in the doorway, papers in hand.

"Are ya'll ready to present your cases?

"Yes, ma'am."

"Got to get to work, Clyde. Catch you later."

The students presented to Trish, and she went with each to see their patients firsthand and then returned to her office after signing the prescriptions to await the presentation of their next cases. Tilting back in her chair, she put her feet up on a pulled-out desk drawer and closed her eyes.

What could be the connection between those two? And where did that clinical trial reject disappear to? Is there any connection to the body on the beach with the blue heart tattoo? And the Weasel hitting on Mi Ling? Could he be involved somehow? He doesn't seem secretive, though. Always running his mouth, but that could be a smoke screen. Who from the Med School bought those puffer fish? Is there a connection? There are just too many unanswered questions. What to do? What to do?

Trish frowned as the thoughts drifted through her mind. Suddenly, she sat up and opened her eyes, and said out loud, "Bacteria! That's what one of those articles said. Bacteria that live in puffer fish actually produce the toxin. It would be easy to culture bacteria and produce a supply of tetrodotoxin. Shoot, most anyone could do that in the corner of a lab and it never be noticed."

"Talking to yourself again, Dr. Trish?"

"Oh, hi, Max, just thinking out loud. How's the world of child protection these days?"

Max, a child protection caseworker, had brought a kid to the clinic for therapy.

"Damn hostile. I think it's like combat duty."

"You're hopefully saving a child."

"I hope so. Sometimes it seems we're just spinning our wheels. I must be having a spell of burnout. I need to go fishing. What's that I heard you talking about, puffer fish? Those are trash fish. I always throw them back."

"So, you're a fisherman?"

"Of sorts. It does relax me a bit and gets my mind off work".

"I heard a fellow was buying puffer fish a while back. You ever hear of that?"

"No, and I can't imagine why anyone would. Fish stew made from them would kill a fellow real quick like. I'd better go see if my kid is finished with his session. Good to see you."

❋

The afternoon at the Clinic ran smoothly, and Trish was able to leave on time. As she drove to the Medical School, she once again let thoughts drift through her mind. *Seemingly unconnected…puffer fish…tetrodotoxin…bacteria…tattoos… cardiac arrthymia…respiratory failure…how did the poison get in those women? Was there anything other than being young, Asian, and having the blue heart tattoo?*

As she pulled into the parking garage at the Medical Center, she slammed on her brakes and said out loud, "Salad fragments! Lettuce! They both had salad fragments in the gastric contents. How could salad be poisoned?"

Another bit of information added to the figure of the mystery and Trish knew that when enough seemingly unrelated items were brought together, a new gestalt would emerge pointing to who did it and why the women were killed.

I must be patient, and patience is a virtue I have in short supply.

❀

THIRTY-THREE

The kids in bed asleep, toys and clutter picked up and stashed, Trish collapsed on the sofa beside Steven.

"It beats me how quickly things get messy. Mercedes hasn't been gone more than three hours, and it looked like a hurricane had come ashore."

"We have two little busy people who are skilled at making a mess, don't we? At least they're active and curious. Too bad there's not a way to harness that energy. How's your week going? Not thinking about the poor girl whose body you found, are you?"

"A little, and when my gal gang got together, I must admit, we discussed it. Let me bring you up to date." Trish told Steven all that had transpired and that McInnis informed the authorities as to cause of death.

"Does that mean you all are bowing out, I hope?"

"Not completely. Coming back from The Mental Health Clinic, I realized something both had in common."

"What was that?"

"They both had salad fragments in their gastric contents. I couldn't figure how salad could be a source for the poison. So, I re-read some of the information I dug up on tetrodotoxin, and guess what?"

Steven kissed Trish on the forehead, smiled and said, "Educate me."

Trish grinned. "Don't be distracting me. I read it was soluble in diluted acetic acid."

"So?" Steven replied as he began to gently rub the back of her neck.

"So, what is vinegar? It's acetic acid! And what's in most salad dressings? Vinegar! They could have ingested it via salad dressing. It would only take a few milligrams."

"Do you think that's what happened?"

"It's certainly a plausible method!" said Trish as he unbuttoned her blouse.

"All right; enough of that. It's beddie-bye-time for us."

"I'm not complaining, Prince Charming. Lead the way." And he did.

Later, as they were drifting off to sleep, Steven said, "That's a great way to end every day."

"How about most, not every," whispered Trish. "We can make up with quality for quantity."

THIRTY-FOUR

"Hello?"

"Hi, Helen. It's me. Where's the old 'Smithe residence, lady of the house' bit?" asked Trish.

"I gave up on that. It started sounding pretentious to me."

"I'll admit, I thought that myself. Glad you let it go. Say, I was thinking. Would you go with me to visit Felicia's mom? And maybe we can look around the area and get some more information about Felicia's friends or acquaintances?" Trish continued loading the Saturday morning breakfast dishes as she spoke, "Remember, we're having a gal meeting here next Saturday."

"Do you want to go today?"

"Sure. Think it's okay to bring the kids? Steven's gone fishing." "Of course. Felicia's baby is just a little younger than Amy. I don't think Felicia's mom would mind."

"I'll pick you up about 10:30. That way, I can give the kids a snack and a late lunch and not miss nap time. They're both little monsters if they miss their little afternoon nap."

"I'll be ready. Just honk and I'll hear you."

It was a pleasant day. Not hot — sunny and with a slight breeze — when Trish pulled into Helen's drive, promptly at 10:30.

As they drove with several twists and turns, Trish said, "Good thing you're giving directions. I don't think I would have found the place. No wonder it took so long for the emergency vehicle to find the place."

"I thought I knew most every little pig trail in these parts, but I never knew about these houses. They're all on stilts, so it must flood a lot down here. There's the house."

The small ramshackle, unpainted house — actually more of a shack — was neat and tidy with plants in tin cans and plastic shortening buckets lined up along the porch edge, their variegated greens softening the otherwise stark and bleak environment. Helen rang a bell on the banister at the foot of the steps. A petite Vietnamese woman with graying black hair opened the front door. Upon recognizing Helen, she smiled broadly and said, "Come in. Good, you brought friend."

Adam in hand and Amy on her hip, Trish struggled up the worn steps behind Helen, who, at the top, had opened her arms wide to embrace the tiny woman.

"So good of you to come," said Mrs. Cheekwood as she returned the hug. "Thank you so for your prayers. I'm feeling much better. Please, come in."

"This is my friend, Trish McLeod, and these are Adam and Amy."

"How do you do? Nice to meet you."

"Thanks. We hope we aren't a bother?"

"No, please, I'm alone most of the time now with Felecia gone." Her face saddened as she dabbed the corner of her eyes with her flower-print apron. "Let me fix you some tea and a cookie for the little ones."

"We don't mean to be any trouble…," started Trish as little Adam said "Cookie please" She relented and took a seat with Amy in her lap.

As Mrs. Chekwood prepared the tea, excusing that she had only tea bags, Helen asked how she had been doing.

"It's been hard. And having the baby to care for, in a way, has given me something to do and not keep thinking about how Felicia died. Thank you for your prayer, and my church people pray for me. Somehow, I feel more peace in my heart. You understand? Baby is asleep now. He'll wake in a little while and play with your boy, eh? Felicia's husband come back in two months and he want baby to stay with his sister. She has two small children. I not so sure; maybe best child need more than one old widow grandmother."

"I'm sure you'll do what's best," said Helen as she sipped her cup of tea." We wanted to ask you a few questions about your daughter, if you don't mind. Did you hear that they discovered a poison in her body and that's why she died?"

"It was a few days back when a nice policeman although he didn't wear a uniform came and told me. He did have a badge, and I look to be sure he is what he say. How she got that? He said it was very quick, maybe only an hour after. Asked me if she was depressed or talked of suicide. Not my girl. She good Christian. Changed her ways."

"Changed her ways, Mrs. Cheekwood? What do you mean by that?" asked Trish.

"Oh, before, when she in her late teens, she ran with a bad group. This before she met her husband. He a good boy, too."

"Bad group? How so?" quizzed Helen.

"I not sure; it was a secret group. That when she got that heart tattoo on her neck. I never approve of it, but when she met husband, and join his church, she change back to old self, like when she was a girl. Even told me she saving money to have tattoo removed. Lady, her boss at the beauty supply shop, knew a place that would take it off with, how you say… laser? A skin doctor over in Mobile."

"Do you think she was using drugs?" asked Trish.

"I don't think so. She never smoked cigarettes or drink beer that I know about. That beer and cigarettes what killed her papa at such an early age. The policeman," she stopped to retrieve a card from a stack of papers on a side table, "Bill Swanson, his name, he ask many questions. I don't think my answers helped him. He ask if he could look around the house. I let him."

As Trish surveyed the sparse surroundings one medium-sized room that served as both kitchen and living room and an open door to a hall, with another open door beyond to a bathroom, she gathered there must be bedrooms off the hall also. *It wouldn't take long to look around here.* A threadbare sofa and recliner, covered with a brightly-colored, crocheted afghan, faced a small TV on a metal stand. A rocker with a floral cushion, a small coffee table, and side table completed the furniture. The kitchen alcove consisted of what Trish called an apartment-sized gas stove, a tiny refrigerator and chrome-and-yellow dinette set right out of the 1950's. A skirt of bright floral print surrounded the kitchen sink. A few toys peeped out of a plastic washtub adjacent to a high chair. Her mama would have labeled it dirt poor but proud, as it was tidy and sparkling clean.

"Did he look in your refrigerator?" asked Trish.

"Why, yes, he did. I thought that unusual and asked if he wanted something to drink, but he said "No.""

"Did your daughter have any enemies, or merely someone who disliked her?" asked Helen.

"Not that I knew of. She didn't have a big bunch of friends — the ladies at her work and a couple in her Sunday school class. She was well loved."

"What about someone from her past?"

"I have no reason to think anyone would want to hurt her, Ms. Helen."

"Did the detective policeman go down to the water out back?" asked Trish.

"No, just the house."

"Would you mind if we took a look?" asked Trish.

By this time, Amy was happily rocking in Mrs. Cheekwood's arms and Adam was exploring the toys in the tub.

As they clambered down the twelve steps to the damp, narrow trail that led to the stagnant water's edge, Helen said, "Why are we going down here? It looks snaky to me."

"Don't worry. Make noise and any snakes will run away."

"What about alligators?"

"Them, too. Don't think there's any around here, though."

"Ugly! This is an overgrown jungle. No wonder the cop didn't come down here."

The footpath gave way to an open space without underbrush near the edge of the water. To one side was a shed-like affair with a slanted roof made of rusted corrugated tin sheltering an apparent fish-cleaning table complete with sluice leading to the water and a water hose nearby.

"How'd they have running water, Trish?"

"Look, this garden hose runs back toward the house. Bet there's an outside faucet there."

"There's no boat, but this looks as if one has been pulled up here out of the water. There's a ring on this tree and wire around the tree."

"See anything else of interest?"

"Hey! What's this?" Helen spied a white Styrofoam box, approximately twelve inches square, lodged in weeds at the waterside.

"Aren't you the brave one? I thought you were afraid of snakes? I don't think I'd put my hand in there," said Trish, as Helen plucked the box from the muck.

"I only wanted to see what it was. Want to open it?"

"No, you. If anything is in there, it's probably rotten."

"Okay, I'll do it."

"Hey, let's be careful. Set it on the table and use these sticks." Helen pried the box open with the stick Trish supplied. It popped open, emitting a foul stench.

"I told you so. Phew! That odor would gag a maggot. What's in there?"

"Several rotten shrimp shells and remains of a salad. This is gross!"

"Don't touch it!"

"Don't worry, I wasn't planning to." Using the stick, she re-closed the lid. Trish pulled several tissues from her pocket and picked up the box gingerly.

"What're we doing now?"

"A hunch I have. Maybe we can get someone to look at this?"

"Why?"

"I'd rather wait to share that with you in case I'm being foolish and dramatic. We need to be going home. I won't leave you in the dark. Promise."

As they drove home, Adam piped from the backseat, "I like that lady."

"Me, too, Champ, and so did Amy," said Trish, noting Amy was already asleep in her car seat.

"Why'd you put that box in a plastic grocery bag and way in the back?"

"In case — the wildest 'in case' — there is something dangerous in it."

❁

THIRTY-FIVE

"You're really pushing the envelope, Trish. I'm not sure I can get my buddies to run another assay. It's a tricky assay to run.

"Look, Barb, I've already discussed it with McInnis. He thinks I'm a nosy nut anyway, but said my hypothesis was plausible, so, indulge me."

"All right. As I say, nothing ventured, nothing gained. The HPLC was for minute amounts of tetrodotoxin."

"No. Do the assay first and then we'll turn the information over to McInnis if it's positive."

"Will do. And I'll tell them to keep the results under their hat."

❋

THIRTY-SIX

The Lunch Bunch munched on Helen's now famous chicken salad on whole wheat toast the following Saturday. The large house sparkled, and Helen fluttered around the table like a bird in mating season.

"Sit down, Helen. Everything is perfect," said Trish.

"Everybody have enough? Here's the peach iced tea. I've already sweetened it; not sugar, though."

"I notice when we're obsessing individually, and as a group, we meet more than once a month," commented Clare. "Not that I'm complaining, especially since one of us has turned into a gourmet chef; or should it be cheftess?"

"Helen and I wanted to hear what Barb got from the HPLC on the food remains we found behind Felicia's house, and we wanted us all to be in on it from the start. So, shoot, Barb." Trish took a bite of fruit salad, dipped it in the poppy seed dressing in the small cut glass dish that was originally designed as a finger bowl.

"First of all, the techs want ya'll to know this was an altruistic act of friendship because part of the remains were from shrimp. The contents smelled to high heaven. Everyone, hold on to your hats: there was tetrodotoxin present. A lot!"

"Wow! Was I in danger from opening the box?"

"No, Helen. You have to ingest it, so we weren't at risk just looking," said Trish.

"But, the smell."

"That was from the rotten shrimp shells," said Clare.

Trish continued. "I went ahead and turned the data over to McInnis as well as the Styrofoam box."

"Remember, there was a box of salad remains in Mi Ling's study nook in the library. I wonder if that was checked for anything?" added Trish.

"There was no reason to. At that point, poison wasn't even a consideration," replied Barb.

"Barb, you know more about this than we do. Could a killer give his victim minute amounts of the poison over time, similar to the manner arsenic poison murderers do," asked Clare?

"Sure, if the killer had lab resources and diluted it down enough; a larger dose would kill quickly, maybe in an hour," said Barb." I've read cases of sushi poisoning where death occurred in twenty minutes."

"At the time I had coffee with him and David at school, Mi Ling's fiancé said she had been feeling fatigued. He thought she was stressed out, working too much," said Trish.

"That could have been because of poison, not work."

"Right on," added Clare.

"Now, how are Mi Ling and Felicia connected? Both are dead from a relatively rare poison. Put your brains together and think outside the box."

"Are we sleuthing again, Trish?"

"Yes, we are, Helen, honey."

"There were salad remains near where both deaths occurred."

"And tetrodotoxin is soluble in diluted acetic acid, so the likely vehicle was salad dressing. Agreed?"

"Sure looks that way to me, and they both had the same tattoo."

"Both were planning on having the tattoo lasered off and both were relatively new converts to Christianity."

"So, maybe it was a symbol of membership in some occult group," replied Clare.

"Certainly it's an unusual mark," added Barb.

"Had Felicia ever been to the Far East? Hong Kong or Thailand or Vietnam?" said Helen.

"We can check on that," said Trish. "Her mama would know. If she had, she didn't get the money for a ticket from her mama. She looks poor as a church mouse. Helen, since Mrs. Cheekwood likes you and you have somewhat of a relationship with her, will you check on that for us?"

"My pleasure. I like her. She's not that old, maybe only in her late sixties. I was hoping to assist her in getting a paying job, so that will be my excuse for another visit."

"Bet she could work in your catering business, Helen," said Clare.

"For sure. Susie was saying we needed another worker."

"They were both religious. Do we know exactly what church they went to? Possibly, the same one? Barb, would you check on that for us?" asked Trish.

"I'm jumping the gun, gals, but I vote for Dr. Weasel as the killer. He's such a twerp," said Clare, "And the combination of jealousy and lust — he'd call it love — can be a motive to kill. Of course, we don't have a connection between him and Felicia."

"We need to know who brought the salad dressing to the victims? Or, did the killer put the poison on the dressing and then somehow get them to eat the salad?" said Helen.

"I'm chatting with a guy who works in the Deli at school. I can ask him if he remembers Mi Ling or if she ate there for lunch," added Barb.

"I don't think either one was expecting poison. They may have feared harm, but eating a salad is an innocent behavior and then, it would be too late to call for help," said Trish.

"From what I've read, the victim could hear and see right up to the point of death and not be able to speak. Remember, all Felicia said was that her tongue was tingling, then she fell down and died," added Helen.

"Do you think they both knew a secret and were murdered out of fear they would reveal it?"

"Hey, that's an idea! What kind of secret?"

"Haven't the vaguest."

"If that's the case, is there any connection between Dr. Weaver and Felicia?"

"None we know of at this point. You know at least one of his techs; see what you can dig up as to what he does outside the lab and school."

"And, not to sound dramatic, but we all should be very careful. There is a killer out there who has access and has used a horrible, potent poison of which only a few milligrams could kill again. And, if he, or she thinks any of us is getting too close may strike again," consoled Clare.

"I say, let's be as discreet as possible, and turn over anything we find to that Detective Swanson and let the police handle it," said Barb.

"Trish, you've talked to him several times. You should be the one to call him," added Helen.

"I'll call if we think we really have something to tell, but not until then. I feel stupid and put down by him anyway, so let's not be premature with this."

The group agreed for Trish to relay any pertinent information to Detective Swanson and at Trish's insistence, jotted down their assignments.

"Oooh, this is so exciting, sleuthing again."

"Cool it a little, Helen. This could be dangerous — a lot more dangerous than a sex club we found Hilda to be part of — even though her death was gruesome," said Trish.

"I'll not eat any salad dressing and only squeeze lemon juice on my salad for a while," said Helen.

"Say, Helen, that may be kooky, but it may be a good preventive measure for all of us," said Trish. "If the killer, or killers, thinks one of us is getting too close, we might be in danger. After all, these cases were written off as deaths by natural causes until we got those tox studies performed."

"I told those guys to keep it quiet," said Barb.

"I know you did, but McInnis gave the information, too.

And the way people gossip, the cat's out of the bag. Wouldn't surprise me if someone in the media got wind of it."

"Trish, those notes you received; any connection?" said Clare.

"I sure hope not. That thought really makes me nervous. Ya'll keep your eyes and ears open and keep thinking. I'm at a loss. Damn! Why does God put these kinds of things in my path?"

"Ever think it's where He wants you to be? How He wants to use you?"

"This just isn't my ball of wax."

"Out of earthen vessels…"

"Oh, don't quote scripture to me now, Helen."

"My house for Lunch Bunch next time," said Barb. "Can we make it in a couple of weeks? I've a lot on my plate right now. Everybody agree?"

"Okay by me," three replied in unison, with Trish adding "We can always call a meeting if necessary. This should give everyone time to do their assignments. I can bounce some of it off Clyde, who I'm more comfortable with, than Detective Swanson."

THIRTY-SEVEN

Early the next week another note appeared in Trish's campus mail. Same block letters, same message: MIND YOUR OWN BUSINESS. The skin on the back of her neck tingled as fear crept into her throat. She whispered under her breath, "Jesus, I don't need this now." On an impulse, she left the note on the floor where it fell, retrieved a Ziploc plastic bag from her desk drawer, and picking the note up with a tissue, dropped it into the bag.

Can't be too careful. It is possible to lift fingerprints from paper.

You've been watching too many crime TV investigations.

But, what if it is connected? At the very least, this is a form of harassment.

Then, out loud, she angrily exclaimed, "I don't have to put up with this shit." Sitting down at her desk, she called Steven at his office and related what happened and her reaction.

"You're right, honey. Will do. Today, you think? All right, I'll leave early."

Trish next called Clare, asking for clinical coverage that afternoon, filled out a leave slip, and turned it into Martha.

"This is a little unusual for you, Dr. Trish. Not feeling well?"

"No, I have some personal family business to attend to. I'll be back tomorrow."

❋

THIRTY-EIGHT

Steven met Trish at the kitchen door when she arrived home. A stress-filled afternoon of frantic packing and driving the kids eighty miles to Steven's brother had left her exhausted.

"You okay?"

"I'm not so sure," said Trish as her husband put his arms around her and kissed her on the forehead.

"I even fixed us a late supper: barbeque chicken, dirty rice and a nice salad with dressing on the side, the way you like it."

"That's sweet of you. I haven't much appetite. I waited until the kids were asleep before I left. Thank God for relatives. They were thrilled to have them, even with Adam not quite potty trained."

"They'll have a great time. After all, they are more experienced parents than we are, and I must admit, I'm somewhat relieved to have them out of the house for a while with those notes and you gals nosing into yet more murder."

"Don't fuss at me, Steven. I feel bad enough." Trish sat in her swivel rocker, took a deep breath, sniffed, took a tissue and blew her nose as tears welled up in her eyes.

"I'm not fussing, honey. I'm just concerned for all our safety. There is a killer out there and you gals uncovered the fact that he or she killed, when before, it would have gone unnoticed."

"Yes, and even if we back off now, he or she will still be exceedingly angry at us, maybe enough to kill again!" Trish rubbed Skip's ears as he put a paw on her knee and laid his head on it. "Sometimes, I wish I wasn't so curious."

"Being curious isn't a bad thing, especially, when something good comes of it."

"The only thing good that can come of this is if the killer is caught. Oh, I miss my babies already."

"Come on and eat a little supper with me, then take one of your famous bubble baths and get a good night's sleep. Things will look better in the morning."

"I hope so, but I'm not as sure as you are. I have a feeling in my gut that there is more to come before this is finished."

❁

THIRTY-NINE

As Trish was loading up the next morning, she heard Skip give a long howl from the backyard. Slamming the car door, she exclaimed, "What is wrong with that dog? I've never heard him bay like that."

Re-entering the house and approaching the patio door, she looked out and noticed a dark mass near the side fence. Skip nosed around it. When she opened the door, Skip ran to her and whined, running back toward the large lump that, as she approached, was clearly a dead dog with a string round its neck and an attached piece of paper with the words BUTT OUT BABE.

"Oh, my God!" Trish's hand flew to her mouth and fear clutched her hear, "Come on, Skip. You're going to the vet for the day. I would worry about you all day if I didn't."

Arriving at the Medical School, she wasted no time and immediately called Steven, relating what had happened.

"Could you please go see about it and take it somewhere, to the vet or out to the country and bury it, Steven? Our Skip is at the vet for now."

Relieved at his willing nature to allay her fear, she had hardly replaced the receiver when Clare popped into her office.

"Running a little late for you, aren't you, Trish? I've already enrolled a new subject for the anxiety study. Anxiety dripped out of him like sweat on a humid summer day. Hey, what's the matter? You looked stressed."

Trish told Clare how she had taken the children to the

country and then found the dead dog in her backyard with an attached note.

"And it was a similar message? BUTT OUT BABE this time?" asked Clare.

"Yes, and I'm feeling even more anxious about these notes. Do you think they have anything to do with us discussing the tetrodotoxin deaths?"

"Frankly, I'm afraid it does, but I haven't a clue how."

Trish picked up the phone and called Sheila into the office.

"Close the door."

"Sure, what's up, Dr. Trish?" asked Sheila.

Trish related the last incident and said, "Sheila, think outside the box, anything come to mind that has changed in the routine around your office since I discovered Mi Ling's body?"

Sheila put one hand on her hip and the other on her forehead and closed her eyes for a moment.

"The only thing at all different is there's a different guy delivering campus mail. Alvin is his name. He used to be in Med Com. I saw him down there several times when I was picking up posters for an exhibit. Then, he was working with a photographer. Now, there's a guy who in my opinion crawled out from under a rock, a wet slimy rock to boot."

"There are more than enough of those around. Don't suppose you asked Alvin about his transfer?"

"I did. You know me, Dr. Trish, can't keep my nose out of other people's business. Alvin, in my book, isn't the sharpest knife in the drawer, but not stupid exactly. I felt sorry for him 'cause, even if he was merely a lackey in Med Com, that job has more status than delivering campus mail and packages. He was very closed-mouth. Said he needed a change of scenery."

"What does that mean?"

"Beats me. I don't think he would have left of his own accord. The way things go around here, nothing surprises me anymore."

"Think Kroen, the slime ball photographer, had him transferred?"

"If he did, it was an unrecognized blessing to Alvin. It hasn't been a couple of weeks that I was rushing, as usual, down by the Traffic Control Office, near the Student Lounge, and almost collided with Kroen. I said, 'S'cuse me,' and that twerp said, 'Bitch, get out of my way.' I was floored. Asshole he is for sure."

"Sheila!" Trish admonished.

"Sorry. I'm sure glad, with the advent of PowerPoint; I'm not trooping down to pick up slides every day or two. Now, it's seldom. Only when I have to check on arrangements for a video interview and Dr. Parker wants the setting perfect for the studio set."

"That's right. I forgot about the nice film studios. Since I don't do taped interviews, I haven't frequented that area of the Med School," said Trish.

Clare who had entered the office a few minutes earlier heard Sheila's comments and said, "I agree with what Sheila said. If Kroen didn't do such terrific work, he wouldn't still be working here, but what he does is professional quality. It's his ratty personality keeps him working here and not in commercial film. He did come here from the West Coast. I overheard some secretaries talking about him in the deli. He was putting the make on one of them and she was tempted. Said his oriental features were intriguing. I couldn't believe my ears. He is such a jerk." At this, Sheila departed.

"Forget him. Give me a break, I have better things to do and I must get to what's behind these notes. Sorry to be curt, Clare. I'll call Barb and Helen for a Lunch Bunch meeting this Saturday."

"See ya at Barb's house, then, on Saturday. By the way, is that the sapphire you told me about that Steven gave you?"

Trish's hand went to the hollow of her throat where a heart-shaped sapphire nestled. "Yes. He had a jeweler in New Orleans create the setting. He also researched the previous owner and get this: it was a drug lord in Macås! He had died a mysterious death, and that's how the sapphire came on the market. He used it to pay a debt instead of money. And before him, other owners in India and Sri Lanka used it to pay off their debts in an illegal drug and gambling organization. Who would have thought it? So, do you like it?"

"It's gorgeous! Better than your description. No doubt you noticed it's not exactly the usual heart shape?"

"That appealed to me from the beginning," said Trish as she fingered the stone. "Oh, my God!"

"What now, Trish?"

"I wondered about this shape and those of the blue heart tattoos earlier but the thought slipped my mind. Just a second." Trish reached behind her neck and unfastened the chain and laid the necklace on the desk.

"Lets look at it again more closely, Clare. Notice the shape."

"It's beautiful, and the asymmetrical cut, makes it more so."

"Remind you of anything?"

"We thought so earlier, but now it is clear for sure. It's the same shape as the heart tattoos on Mi Ling and Felicia!"

"Certainly, mon cherie, and how could I have forgotten the similarity? I never realized it, in my conscious mind."

"What's behind that?"

"Did I tell you the dealer said it came from Macås and had a mysterious background? Wouldn't tell us. I think he was afraid we might not buy it. I'm not superstitious that way. I'm so glad Steven researched it."

"I don't remember you telling me that, however, we're acting like nervous Nellies. There is probably no connection. Enjoy wearing it. I would be glad to take it off your hand any-time."

"Thanks, but I think not," replied Trish as she re-fastened the necklace, "Must get to work and cease obsessing over these murders."

"Me, too. My resident and students are waiting in my office by now. See you Saturday at Barb's house." As she arose, a slip of paper fell to the floor from the stack of junk mail on the corner of Trish's desk.

"What's this, Trish? Oh, my God! Look!" The note in block letters read BUTT OUT BITCH OR YOU'LL BE NEXT.

FORTY

As the week progressed, Trish calmed herself with work and no more notes appeared. Steven had taken the dead dog, an apparent stray, to their vet, and to Trish's surprise, asked the vet to take a blood sample and store it before he buried the dog behind a fishing buddy's camp house on Bayou Beouf. Normally, he enjoyed meandering through these lowlands, but today's task made his being there grim.

Trish mulled over the thoughts in her mind as she pulled into the circular drive of Barb's house on Saturday.

"Hi, everybody. You saved me a seat at the head?"

"You are our leader, of sorts."

"It looks that way. I'm the principal priestess of the obsessing cult."

"Anybody need anything?" asked Barb as she placed a plate of quiche and salad in front of Trish and took a seat. "I thought we could talk while we eat, in case some of you have pressing comments."

"With Trish getting those nasty notes and then the dead dog, this is my pressing comment for today."

"Dead dog, Clare?"

"Yep, Helen," and Trish proceeded to fill in the group.

"So, what new data do we have to fill in the ground so a new figure can merge?" asked Trish.

"What's she saying?"

"Not to worry, it's her psychobabble. She wants us to give our reports."

"Oh, I'll go first then. I visited Mrs. Cheekwood. She's such a sweetheart and wants to join my Bible Study Group."

"On with your report."

"Sorry. I was thrilled about that and she is going to work part-time for Susie and me."

"What did she tell you about her daughter?"

"Oh, that. Yes, she did go to Hong Kong about the time she was a senior in high school. Seems some of Mrs. Cheekwood's relatives in Saigon had relocated there and sent a plane ticket and wanted to meet her. And — how did I forget to tell ya'll? — when she came back, she had the blue heart tattoo on her neck. Wouldn't talk about it to her mama. Because she was gone three weeks, she missed graduating with her class. Her mama said she took the GED that summer and passed with flying colors. Girl was real smart; had hopes of a better job than in the beauty supply shop. It was after she married and got pregnant that she joined the church and decided to remove the tattoo."

"And what do you have to report, Dr. Barb?" asked Trish.

"Had a friendly chat with the deli worker, Rosco. Mi Ling did eat lunch there frequently; and usually with Dr. Wesley Weasly Weaver."

"Interesting, but not surprising, as she was his postdoc," said Trish.

"And, check this, Kroen from Med Com joined them on several occasions, but not after Mi Ling became engaged. Rosco observed that he and Weaver seemed like buddies," said Barb.

"That's hard to believe. Weaver is so stuck on himself. Surprises me he'd be friends with a mere photographer from Med Com?" said Clare.

"As far as I can see, they both have ratty personalities. Ever hear birds of a feather flock together?"

Trish continued, "There has to be more. Dr. Weasel must have some other connection. Did he have Kroen making pictures for him?"

"I'd bet on obscene movies — porno stuff — that would appeal to the Weasel."

"Agreed, but Weaver is into power and control big time, and has expensive taste. Porno would be fluff. He goes for a hundred-dollar-a-bottle of wine, remember?"

"Rosco thought Kroen was leaning on Mi Ling a bit, but when she wore her engagement ring, he backed off and stopped eating with them," said Barb.

"Did he notice what they ate?"

"I did ask and Mi Ling always ate salad."

"What kind of dressing?" asked Trish.

"Remember, I'm a toxicologist. He said little tubs of dressing, the kind that pop the cap off. There's more."

"More?" breathed Helen hanging on every word.

"Yep. I talked to one of Mi Ling's roommates. Even bought her lunch. Those Asian girls eat like birds. Anyway, Mi Ling spent a lot, and I mean a lot of time at the Med School. Weekends, nights, too, until she became engaged and joined the church. It was a non-denominational one called Christ's Way."

"That's the one Felicia joined. I forgot to tell ya'll," piped Helen.

"So, there is a connection between the two women."

"Looks that way to me," said Barb.

"Do we know what she was doing at the Med School? The library closes at 10:00 p.m. and is only open after noon on Sunday," said Trish.

"That's a mystery for sure. Her roommate said many times it was after midnight when she came in, and she went some Sunday mornings, early before church, also," said Barb.

"Helen, did you happen to ask Mrs. Cheekwood if Felicia had long, unexplained absences?" asked Trish.

"Not exactly. I did ask if she had any idea why someone would kill her. As a result of that question, she remembered same as Mi Ling. Before Felicia met her husband and became engaged, she did leave for long periods. She didn't know where she went, but a Japanese-looking fellow picked her up in a paneled van."

"Kroen is Japanese."

"Oh, my God. Is he a connection, Trish?"

"It's beginning to look that way. However, connection is not a motive for murder."

"I still say, as before: Weaver is involved. He's a scientist, if not a toxicologist."

"Point taken. I say enough is enough. I'll call Detective Swanson and relate all we have talked about. The situation is getting too creepy for me, and I miss my babies."

"What about the man buying puffer fish and selling them to someone from the Medical School?"

"I'll tell you my idea on that and if it turns out to be the truth, I want accolades from all of you; especially, Miss Curiosity-personified, Dr. Trish," said Clare. The person who bought the fish may not have been from school, only wearing a borrowed white lab coat. I still believe Dr. Weaver is involved. Even though he is a pharmacologist, he has the necessary skill to culture the tetrodotoxin in bacteria, and to purify it without anyone being the wiser."

"Except, Mi Ling may have been suspicious," said Helen.

"However," said Trish, "he did have the hots for her and may have acted nicer to her than it looked to others; and they worked together. In addition to lusting after her, I'll take odds he was jealous as hell of her ideas and research."

"How did he deliver the poison?" asked Helen.

"I read, as I mentioned before, it's soluble in diluted acetic acid. She had salad for lunch. He could have loaded some containers of dressing with the poison, maybe just one milligram at first, making her weak and fatigued. Then, took her a salad with a toxic dose the day he killed her. Kindly assisted her to the stairwell for fresh air and watched her die, unable to speak, gasping for breath."

"That's a horrible, sadistic theory to be sure, and something keeps nagging at the back of my mind that there is more than simply money and power to a connection with Kroen?"

"For true. Does anyone have any ideas about that? They did seem friends or at least friendly."

"Pictures," said Helen again. "Kroen is a photographer. Maybe they were in business together making porn films, and Felicia and Mi Ling were in them and bowed out."

"I think you're grasping at straws," replied Trish, "However, anything is possible, so I'll mention it to Detective Swanson when I talk to him."

"As far as we can tell, Weaver had no connection with Felicia, but Kroen might have."

"Possible, not probable. If they were filming porno, where would they do it?"

"The Med Com studios at night and on weekends?"

"Holy shit! That is an idea that bears further investigation."

"Please let the police do any further investigation."

"Maybe. I will ask Sheila to chat with the secretary in Med Com."

"Trish, please…"

"I'll think about it, Clare."

❀

FORTY-ONE

A jolly birthday party was winding down for Adam, who had turned three. The Lunch Bunch was just sitting down in Trish's den, sipping Mimosas, and Steven was saying good-bye to perky four-year-old Samantha in her frilly blue party dress, big bow askew in her hair, when the doorbell rang. Adam announced, "She's my girlfriend," to the women as he passed through. Who could be ringing that bell this late in the afternoon?

"Come on, Champ. Let's go play with your new toys, and Adam, you are too young for a girlfriend anyway. Let the ladies chat."

For once there was no objection from Adam as he cheerfully led his dad by the hand to the back of the house.

"I'll get the door," Steven called, on his way out of the den.

"Ya'll ever notice how when we are obsessing over a murder, we meet almost every week and then, when the killer or killers, as in the last case, are brought to justice, we only get together sporadically. We waited nine months for Adam's birthday party."

"You're right. Our lives are so busy, and after all that intrigue, we needed a good long break," said Helen.

"Let's make a pact that from now on, we'll lunch regularly, once a month," said Barb.

"I'll make the time if you will."

"Sure," replied Barb, as did Trish and Clare.

"Did you ever find what the heart tattoo was about?" asked Helen.

"It was a sign of membership in a sex cult which required performance of sexual acts as part of the religious experience," answered Trish.

"How gross. This last time we became involved in a murder investigation was too close for comfort, if you ask me. That last note certainly was a direct threat to you," said Barb.

"Yes, I'm glad I called Detective Swanson when I did. He was supportive and nice to me. Said he appreciated all the things we'd discovered and suggested. Too bad it wasn't soon enough to nab ol' Kroen. He had checked out by taking some of his own poison. And damn, to do it in the Med Com studio!"

Just then, who stood in the den doorway and announced himself but that very detective. "Hello, Trish. Ladies. Steven pointed me back here. I'm meeting my partner nearby on a current case we've got, and I've wanted to stop by and speak with you all along the way. I've wanted to talk to you for several months now.

"I realize I can appear abrupt and ungrateful. I excuse myself as being overworked and part of a difficult job. But in the case of Mi Ling's murder and all the others with that funny blue heart, all the work you ladies did was invaluable and, frankly, was the exact turning point that allowed the police to tie all the pieces together and solve the case. If you had not ordered the assays for the two puffer fish poisoned women, the murders would never have been solved.

"Thank you so much, each one of you. The Department wanted you to know how grateful we are. I believe they're planning some kind of awards ceremony soon." Detective Swanson came forward and shook each of their hands and exited as abruptly as he'd come in.

"Well, I swear. I am bowled over right now," said Trish.

"Me, too. Me, too, Me, too," chimed in the others. "Who could ever have anticipated that? It's almost like a handshake of friendship."

"Great idea. Let's think of it like that," said Trish. And

now, where were we? I think we were talking about old Kroen, weren't we?"

"At least he left a note telling us he killed Felicia out of jealousy," Claire chimed in.

"Isn't that the pits? How could he be so jealous when he knew she loved her husband and was moving on to a new life?"

"I think it was a combination of jealousy and loss of power because she was a star in some of his porno films," said Barb.

"Wasn't that a gas? Making them right in the Medical School under the noses of administration," chirruped Helen.

"Good thing Detective Swanson thought to remove some of the ceiling tiles on the drop ceiling in Med Com. That was where most all the film, props, and equipment etc., if you will, were stored."

"And, remember, in his suicide note, it wasn't the poison in the salad that killed Felicia. He got her to drink lemonade in a foam container. She had just eaten lunch, and knowing the time of day she agreed to meet him, he had a back-up plan. He put the poison in something else that was acetic," said Helen.

"I'm surprised she even agreed to go down and meet him," Helen mentioned.

"He told her he realized any possibility of a relationship was over and that he wanted her to have a token gift to remember him by," said Barb.

"If it were me, I wouldn't want to remember what I did. I'd like to delete the memories forever," said Helen.

"I bet she did. However, she was in financial difficulties and may have thought she could sell the gift or pawn it for some much needed cash," said Clare.

"It isn't that uncommon for Japanese men to commit suicide, and this guy knew the possibility of being caught and prosecuted was a near reality. This way, in his twisted thinking, he had the final ultimate control," said Trish.

"Talk about crooked thinking. That takes the cake."

"Lust and jealousy are a powerful combination."

"Mi Ling, a porno star? That's hard to believe."

"Looks that way."

"Yep, and it's the same with ol' Dr. Weasel. It's wonderful what DNA testing can accomplish. He didn't confess; but when Swanson found a medical student who saw him escorting Mi Ling out the door to the stairwell, that really tightened the noose," said Trish.

"What about the stuff they found in his lab," continued Clare. Sure another nail in his coffin. Can you believe he was culturing the bacteria in a corner of his lab?"

"Sometimes people who are brilliant in some ways, do incredibly stupid things otherwise. I have observed more than once," said Barb.

"Think the combination of lust and jealousy blinds the intellect, Trish?"

"Yes, I do. He could have just ordered tetrodotoxin from a supply house. It isn't a controlled substance. And honestly, his threats on those cards were more evidence of his narcissistic personality."

"But a purchase from a supply house could be traced," said Barb.

"What will happen to him, Trish?"

"Helen, as he's still a United Kingdom citizen, I don't think he can be sentenced to death here in this state, but it has been done a couple of times in other states. At the worst, after he serves many years of time here in the States I hope, he'll be deported back to the U.K."

"I can tell ya'll, the powers that be in the Medical School were shaken to the tips of their toes. The very idea of porno films being made in the school's Med Com studios was a shock. Wow!" exclaimed Clare. "That included every one from the Dean on down to the laundry workers."

"And it was horrid and sadistic, giving the gals poison and then watching them die; except, Felicia made it back to the house before she collapsed," mused Trish.

The entire affair was a ninth degree shocker, and all the women agreed in unison that this would be their last venture in solving murder.

Only time would tell.

❋

ABOUT THE AUTHOR

Fran Hagaman is a retired professor of clinical psychiatry, LSU Medical School, Shreveport, and a distinguished fellow of the American Psychiatric Association. She also served as Medical Director of Region 7 Louisiana Mental Health. She is a longtime associate member of the SW Chapter of Mystery Writers of America. Fran lives in Shreveport, Louisiana.

Also Available:

Rub-A-Dub-Dub - Death in a Tub

A Medical Mystery

Trish McLeod mysteries can be ordered
from fine bookstores everywhere.

❋

To contact the author email:
Fran@Hagaman.com